A Warding Circle

Critical Praise for the books of Djelloul Marbrook

Artemisia's Wolf (title story, *A Warding Circle*)

. . . successfully blends humor and satire (and perhaps even a touch of magic realism) into its short length . . . an engrossing story, but what might strike the reader most throughout the book is its infusion of breathtaking poetry. . . a stunning rebuke to notoriously misogynist subcultures like the New York art scene, showing us just how hard it is for a young woman to be judged on her creative talent alone.

—Tommy Zurhellen, *Hudson River Valley Review*

Saraceno

. . . Djelloul Marbrook writes dialogue that not only entertains with an intoxicating clickety-clack, but also packs a truth about low-life mob culture *The Sopranos* only hints at. You can practically smell the anisette and filling-station coffee.

—Dan Baum, author of *Gun Guys* (2013), *Nine Lives: Mystery, Magic, Death and Life in New Orleans* (2009) and others

. . . a good ear for crackling dialogue . . . I love Marbrook's crude, raw music of the streets. The notes are authentic and on target . . .

—Sam Coale, *The Providence (RI) Journal*

. . . an entirely new variety of gangster tale . . . a Mafia story sculpted with the most refined of sensibilities from the clay of high art and philosophy . . . the kind of writer I take real pleasure in discovering . . . a mature artist whose rich body of work is finally coming to light.

—Brent Robison, editor, *Prima Materia*

Alice Miller's Room (title story, *Making Room*)

This enchanting novella is a delicately wrought homage to Jung's famous principle of meaningful coincidence...

—*Breakfast All Day*, UK

. . . the story draws us into that mysterious and terrifying realm where the heart will have its say and all who enter leave transformed...

—Dr. Patricia L. Divine

Mean Bastards Making Nice

I love it. I admire it. It is you at your best.

—Novelist Gail Godwin on "The Pain of Wearing Our Faces"

Guest Boy

. . . it is in books like this that I seek answers and guidance as I travel my own path to enlightenment and contentment. This book opened a struggle in me . . .

—Isla McKetta, editor, *A Geography of Reading*

A Warding Circle

New York Stories

Djelloul Marbrook

LEAKY BOOT PRESS

A Warding Circle
by Djelloul Marbrook

First published in 2017 by
Leaky Boot Press
http://www.leakyboot.com

ISBN: 978-1-909849-21-1

For I. Rice Pereira, my Aunt Irene

Acknowledgments

An earlier version of the title story, "A Warding Circle," was published as *Artemisia's Wolf* by Prakash Books, India, in 2011.

"Yo Scheherazade" was first published in *Orbis* 152 (UK), Fall 2010, and won a *New Millennium Writings* honorable mention in 2007.

"Gatecrasher" was first published in *The Country and Abroad* (Pine Plains, NY), July 2008.

"Ootwaert's Hoe," an except from *Crowds of One*, Book 2 in the *Guest Boy* trilogy, was published in *Prima Materia* Vol. 4, *Speeding Through the Night*, 2005. A somewhat different version, titled "Artists Hill," won the 2008 *Literal Latté* fiction prize and appeared in *Literal Latté*, Fall 2008.

"Return Flight" appeared in *Breakfast All Day* (UK), in issue 10.

"Later for You" was a finalist in the White Eagle Coffee Store long-story competition in 2007.

Contents

A Warding Circle

It stopped my heart, cracked my head, tore my rotator cuff, turned me purple and made my crotch bleed. Just for starters.

I was sitting up in Mercy Hospital in Kingston, New York, studying the gotchas and gizmos around me. Lightning strikes twenty-five million times a year in the United States, the lettuce-green nursie was telling me. It strikes about three hundred people a year, and you're one of them.

"So I won the lottery?"

"Do you remember, dear? Do you remember?"

"Who's this dear? Well, save that for another day. I don't remember a damned thing. I hope it turns out I have a pretty name, one that doesn't wear me out lugging it around."

"You have a lovely name, dear. It's Artemisia Cavelli."

I nod and squint with the pain of it. Do I feel like this name? I don't feel like any name. I don't want one. What an annoyance! I feel left behind. Something moved on and left me behind. What self-respecting person needs a name, anyway?

"Which god raped me?"

"You have a concussion, Artemisia."

"Concussed, so that's it. Sounds familiar."

"Actually, you have a skull fracture. That's why you're all bandaged up. And you have a cut on your forehead. You were in a coma. But don't worry, dear, the doctors say you're going to have a perfect recovery."

A perfect recovery sounds like going backwards to me. I look at my legs, twiddle them a little. Not broken. Toes seem okay, fingers too. That's good. Why is it good? Do I have a special need for them? I really like this question.

"You're tired, dear, we'll leave you alone for now. Rest, everything's all right."

I stare at my fingers. They look as if they're used to doing something wonderful. I like them. Long and articulate. They have a lot of repose. They know how to work and how to rest. What's that trace of cadmium blue in the cuticles? How do I know it's cadmium blue? Do I have a special need for this body or does it need me? Aha, she's a nun, this nurse. I can see the humor in her eyes. She likes my concussion very much, she's enjoying it. I think I'll enjoy it too. We'll have a party. Struck by lightning. How pedestrian. I prefer being raped by Pan. Yes, I'll say I got his goat and he raped me and . . . now what? Let's have a little pregnant pause. Preggo, is that it? I'm going to bear his child, child of light. I'm going to have a little goat-footed demigod? And yes, it's still there, my feathersome crotch. What subject will it bring up next, I wonder. If you're going to be raped, make it Pan. Apollo is full of it. Zeus is passé and Prometheus, well, he's a do-gooder, isn't he? Pan is perfect.

"Did you know, Sister, the only way to keep your balance when you're concussed is to keep your fingers buried in your crotch? It slows everything down."

I lick my gooey fingers and squint at her.

"No, I didn't, dear," she said.

She squints back. Nursie strikes me as someone who's always interrupting gods at their profanities. I have a hunch she's a rather inconvenient nun.

"I'm eager to get back to my break-dancing, maybe a little macarena."

"Don't you do that on your head? You can't do that, dear."

"My head's been spinning since I was born. Actually I was born to make heads spin. Things look better with your feet in the air. My grandmother told me that. I think she got the idea changing my diapers. She must have noticed that I like the way things look."

"You are very pretty, dear, but it's not good to dwell on it."

"I'm pretty beautiful. It's just a fact, it doesn't impress me one way or another, but you can't paint if you're going to call blue

14

black. I paint, you know. That's what this cadmium blue in my cuticles is about. One thing you have to know about beautiful, it isn't good for you. Oh, maybe a few people here and there are generically beautiful the way Lord Byron had a consensually beautiful face. But real beauty goes around calling up dangerous ideas and smelling funny. Lots of people look at me and think, She's beautiful, but only a relative few get twitchy about it, like Pan. When my blond Lombard father and my red-haired Scots mother got into it they made a gray-eyed redhead. Not bad for two narcissists, but a bit stagey. What the hell will Pan and I make? I don't think he gives a shit. I think it's up to me. I think I'll give him an ogre. What would you think of a little red ogre, Sister?"

"Take a deep breath, dear. You mustn't talk like that. I mean, the words are just fine, but you sound ratty-tat-tat."

She takes a deep breath to show her patient. She holds her palms just under her breasts, orchestrating a deep breath. Artemisia watches her breasts rise and winks. It hurts the gash on her forehead and she winces.

Nursie and the handsome young doctor who looks hangdog about being German think I'm making a strange recovery. They've been in to see me twice this morning. The hospital is probably combing my insurance to see if I can pay for psychiatric help. They keep giving me tests.

"Do you know who's president, dear?"

"Yes, the Supreme Court elected the missing link and is boarding him in the White House. No, I'm not going to say that blot looks like a butterfly. I think it looks like my vagina. I do know my birth date. I've always been outrageous, it's nothing new, but only when provoked. I want you to fix up my body and let me out of here, which is the reason I'm talking about Pan. You have no idea who's nuts and who's not, and neither do I, but I think we both suspect the nuts are in charge."

"Artemisia, yoohoo, Artemisia, there's a gentleman here who says he's your husband. You didn't say you were married, dear. Artemisia?"

"I hear you. No, I didn't say. I wouldn't say. Why would I?"

15

There you go, following my eyes to the darkest corner of the room. It worries you, my eyes wandering when you say something you think is important. You think maybe I'm concocting an answer, prestidigitating out of my right brain. You haven't noticed I'm not examining the walls, I'm looking at something in the corner of the room, something sitting watchfully, looking back at me. I notice that you haven't noticed. I think it's because you don't see him. But I do, and you're not going to get an answer out of me until I get an answer from him. You do notice, don't you, my lips are not moving?

"Artemisia, dear, what shall I tell him? They won't let him up if you're not ready to see him. He's quite insistent, though. He's talking about his rights."

"Rights? Now you've got my attention, little sister. Here's a Bronx cheer for his rights. Nobody has any rights with me. Haven't you noticed my eyes are gray? You do remember Athena, don't you? That's the stuff, sister, let's stick together on this issue of male rights. You just chuckle yourself down to the reception desk and tell him Athena is indisposed, and that's good for him, because he definitely doesn't want her full attention."

"All right, Artemisia, I get it. Don't go on so. You'll pop your stitches."

"I'm glad you do—get it, I mean, because I don't. Who the hell is he? Whoa, wait a minute, did you do a rape kit on me?"

"Artemisia, the EMTs brought you here after you were hit by lightning. You're not a rape victim, dear."

"How do you know, did you look?"

"I'm sure they did, dear. I'm sure they examined you to a fare-thee-well."

"You're putting me on, aren't you?"

"I'm glad you're feeling better."

"Yeah, I'm just kidding. I was imagining what a rape kit might turn up if I'd been raped by a god, you know, one of those Greeks, not your kind of god, he's too big. How're they gonna identify Pan's DNA?"

"Artemisia, you must have been a handful, you *are* a handful. What an imagination. Zeus and his thunderbolts and all that."

"Yeah, and all that, Sister. Oh, and about this husband and his rights, maybe you could tell him that my amperage has been significantly upgraded and he can't put anything in my sockets any more. No, sister, you can chuckle, but you can't smirk."

"Your poor mother, dear, how did she cope?"

"She didn't, she gave me to her mother and we spent my whole childhood laughing."

"Really, dear? You had a lovely childhood then?"

"Yes, we did, but it was interrupted by Haley's death. Haley was my grandmother. She was more like my sister. She died and left me a ton of money. Did I ever tell you that?"

"No, dear, but I'm sure the business office will be glad to hear it."

"Yes, I'm stinking rich. That must be why what's-his-face is here, don't you think?"

"So you do remember him, Artemisia?"

"He's probably generic, but sure, I remember him."

Like hell. I have the voltage of a god animating me, what would I do with an earthling? But I better fake this whole mess out or I'll never get out of here. My usual vivid palette is back. I look as if I use rouge. And I'm brushing my teeth fanatically, always a good sign. The husband or whatever he is can wait, damned if I know for what. I should get his name. It's not going to be Cavelli. That was my father's name. What I really need to do is find out how Pan re-engineered me. Why do I remember some things and not others? Why was he picky when he threw out pieces of my hard disk? Picky, picky Pan. I just remembered I don't know what happened, I just know what they told me. Maybe the lightning blew my cortex. Do you think you could bring your unblinking sapphires over here and lick my face or some other part of me, if you wish? Do you think you could stop staring? I'm not complaining about our lack of conversation. I know you've been telling me a lot, and I appreciate it, I do. But don't you think you're editing the tape a bit too much? I mean, what the hell happened? I know the EMTs brought me here, but I don't know from where. I've been doing a lot of listening, like always. It's what I do. You've been doing a lot of talking, or whatever it is you do to put thoughts in my head. But a straight linear account would be nice. Or perhaps a few random facts. For example, where do I live? Yeah, right, my license has an address and my insurance card is traceable, but the damned address doesn't mean a thing to me. Number Two Sutton Place. Nice address. I can picture it. I'm a New Yorker, but I can't picture me in it. They buy paintings at Number Two Sutton Place, they don't paint them. Now what kind of continuity editing is that?

Yes, all right, I know, Paul Cézanne reduced everything to its essential shape, so what I know right now is all that's essential. Have I got that right? I do? Okay, so we're not going to reinvent the Salon. I know what I need to know, it doesn't matter if part of the canvas is bare. The new Artemisia doesn't need any detail, any decor. She's a Cézanne version of her old self. No frame, no varnish, some bare canvas . . . oi, my nipples itch. They're nice, you'd have to admit. Who'd have to admit? Do you like them? You're not interested? I'm going to leave you here if you're not more accommodating. What do I want you to accommodate? Well, see, that's a pretty good question, because I don't know enough about me to answer you. I'm sorry I threatened you. I won't leave you here. If you're foolish enough to follow me, you can come. You might as well, since I'm the only one who sees you. I don't think you need me. Have I got that right? Hmm, I thought so. Did Pan send you here?

"Doctor Haeckel, with everything she's endured I'm reluctant to bring this up, but . . ."

"So?"

"Well, whenever I prod her memory she stares into a corner of the room and I notice she never blinks. We're supposed to blink, Doctor. Sometimes she's a chatterbox, sometimes she feels no obligation to answer me at all. And when I leave the room and linger outside I hear her talking to someone. But there's no one there."

"Yes, yes, of course. Which corner, may I ask?"

"That's interesting, Doctor, because it's always the same corner, just to the right as you walk in. It's the darkest corner."

not saying likes me more than she should because more's okay with me—you could say she might be spying on me and I'm just assuming that it's her over there on Big Momma's right wrist. But you wouldn't be right, because Artemisia Cavelli sees Sister Claudine's face, just like I had her in the cross-hairs of a high-powered rifle. She's taking notes. I don't know how good her eyesight is. If I showed her my gala boobs, could she see them? The thought crosses my mind, but I wouldn't do that, I wouldn't mock her that way, because she's a lovely person. Would the old Artemisia mock her that way? Would the old Artemisia know Sister Claudine's heart? It may be necessary to leave the old Artemisia in a Mercy dumpster with the medical debris. Okay, Sister, you stay there and take notes. I'll behave. Now, as for what's going on down there in the parking lot, well, there's a dark green '54 D-Type Jaguar down there with all the necessaries, including a blonde with cardiac-arrest calves bending over the hood. Why is she bending over the hood? Reading a map maybe, fixing to give Big Momma's cardiac unit more business with those calves. Here comes Mr. D-Type, wearing a white suit, and I think it's after Labor Day, so he's probably an arriviste because nobody with any class wears white after Labor Day, unless of course he hasn't changed his suit in several days. Why's he chucking his left thumb behind him at Big Momma? Ah, La Blonde turns, folds the map and stares belligerently at D-Type. Why belligerent? Has he been visiting his mater? Ah, mater's got the moolah, so she has to be visited. I don't know how you can be gorgeous with your mandibles jutting like that, must have been an English bulldog in another life. Type D is excitable. He's chucking that thumb like a hitchhiker. He'd be welcome in exclusive clubs, turning acquisitive heads, blowing mater's money. Definitely a tennis type, mmm, polo maybe, or jai alai. They're made for each other. Wait a second, maybe they're brother and sister. Ooo, that would be spicy. Brother and sister, lovers too. Sure do look it. And boy, is he pissed. They bring out the prurient in me, this erotic couple. I bet it's what they do best, I bet it's all they do. I don't think I'd like them, but what's liking got to do with it? And what is *it*? The fact they make me think of my crotch or . . . Hey, how about this? D–Type is here to see me. He's Artemisia's husband and La Blonde is his girlfriend. But I like her better as his sister. Yeah, that's what I like her for. There's that ammoniac connection between them. I can smell it from here. The precious bouquet of incest. Well, come to think of it, Artemisia, you could have it both ways: he could be your husband and she could be your sister-in-law. Do you paint nudes? You'd surely have liked to paint her. But would you have married a Type D? You know, girl, this may be the first time you've had a real head on your shoulders. You might have been a jerk, a beautiful red-haired, gray-eyed jerk. Do jerks come in those flavors? Artists are prejudiced, always confusing beauty and truth. I think a jerk in those flavors would have been some piece of work. Especially if her name was Artemisia Cavelli. And D–Type? He most certainly would have been attracted to a jerk, especially if she tolerated Sis. Hell, she might have more than tolerated Sis. Now that's a thought. You know, this being struck by lightning is fun. Pan, you definitely would approve of such a ménage, wouldn't you, you old goat? Oh yes, you played your pipes for the three of us, didn't you? But there's just one problem with him being the husband. He's a Vogel, and Artemisia, even the old Artemisia, wouldn't have married anybody named Vogel. Yes, he's a Peter Vogel, I'm sure of it. Now Cardiac Calves there, she probably didn't have a choice. That's her cross to bear, she's a beautiful Vogel, a contradiction in terms. So what's their game?

"Artemisia dear, do you feel up to him? I can put him off a little while longer, but sooner or later we've got to deal with him, don't you think?"

"Sister Claudine, dear Sister Claudine, I like you better in your green scrubs. What're you wearing under your scrubs? I'm not going to deal with anybody named Vogel. Ever. You can stick your thermometer in my mouth, you can stick it in my little heinie, but I'm not going to entertain a Vogel."

"What makes you think the gentleman's name is Vogel, dear? I didn't tell you that."

"Because if he isn't, he ought to be. I can't deal with a Vogel.

21

A Sturdevant perhaps. Bring me a Schuyler Sturdevant with a long nose and pokey elbows. A vogel sounds like a . . . an oompah."

"I think you're thinking of a flugelhorn, dear. A vogel sounds a little like a flugel. I'll get some papers, Artemisia, we'll try to find out a little more and then you and I will talk about it, about him."

"You mean we'll just postpone him long enough to see how crazy I am. Then he can visit me in the back ward. Will you visit me, too, Claudine?"

"Listen, Artemisia, if you want to get rid of Mr. Vogel or whatever his name is, this is not the way to do it. I don't think you're crazy. I think you're dotty, daft, like most of us nuns and lots of other people. About the lightning, well, I don't know. I know about the Dannion Brinkley case. But I imagine you were a perfectly wonderful girl before you were hit by lightning, and he wasn't a perfectly wonderful person, was he? The thing is, dear, you don't want to give the psych people an excuse to detain you, and you don't want to give Mr. What's-His-Name an excuse either. You see where I'm going with this? You need to rein in your natural exuberance so we can get you out of here. I know you like to tease me. I do. I like it too. I like you. I'm not blind. I see what's going on. We like each other in several different ways, but we have to get you out of here. So I don't want to co-operate with Mr. Vogel or whoever he is. Do you really not know who he is, dear?"

Sister Claudine was staring intently at Artemisia.

"I wouldn't have let him put anything in me, would I?"

"Well, we were all young and silly once, Artemisia. Perhaps you had your reasons. Perhaps he's actually nicer than he seems to be. He's distraught, that's all I can tell."

"Have you met him, Sister Claudine?"

"We've encountered each other, I would say, yes."

"And did you find him a little rubbery?"

"Oh Artemisia, what in the world do you mean by that?

"You know, odd-smelling, like burning rubber, kind of tricky. I'm sure you know what I mean."

"I don't believe he was the kind of boy I would have invited into my bedroom before I put on the habit, if that's what you mean."

"Well, that's a good answer. What about La Blonde? Would you have invited her?"

"Well, I don't think she's your handy-dandy all-purpose thin-nosed blonde, if that's what you mean. Actually she seems frightened."

"Ah, not the prep school girl with the circle pin, the one we all despaired of being?"

"No, Artemisia, in fact I think she's quite mad and that you would like her, assuming, that is, you don't already know her."

"And already slept with her, you mean?"

"I didn't say that, Artemisia. I'm not the stereotype you think I am. I don't think the way you seem to think I think. I like you very much, which is why I wish you'd let me help you get out of this before you're bushwhacked."

I do like this nursie. Bushwhacked in Big Momma's arms? Yes, that's where we all get bushwhacked. I'm really not myself, whoever myself is, and I should listen to Sister Claudine. I'm not myself and haven't a clue who I ought to be, so I should just let this foxy nun get me out of here. Where, I don't know, but one step at a time I always say. Do I always say that? I have no idea what I always say, but I do know life seems a lot more do-able than it did before lightning struck. Before it struck there was something totally not do-able. Life seems hilarious. And I'd like to see what I can do on canvas now that I'm different. I don't know what the brain scan will show, but I'll bet my heels are about to sprout little wings. That's it, I felt like I was walking in goo, and now I feel aerial.

"Sister Claudine, can you get me a sketchpad and some different kinds of pencils, maybe some charcoal? Some chalk? The psych people might like to see what I draw."

Sister Claudine looks worried.

"Yes, they might like to, but would that be good? I'll go to the art supply store tomorrow, Artemisia."

"But you're not sure this is a good idea, right?"

"Right. On the one hand I want to see your work, I want to see what you'll draw, but on the other hand . . ."

"You won't pose for me nude?"

"No. I won't."

"Okay, I'll draw you nude anyway. I'm sure I can do it."

"Yes, I'm afraid you can. But I think you better not."

As she slipped out of Artemisia's room Sister Claudine was sure only that Artemisia Cavelli would carry out her latest threat.

May the IRS audit your nihilist face,
lift your passport, freeze your sexual assets
and jerk you around a hundred years.

Nuala Gwilt, terrorist-in-chief of postmodern art by virtue of a genocidal tongue, gemmy if androgynous looks, and a curatorial knack for razzmatazzing museum benefactors, repeated this curse before her morning ablutions for two weeks, more or less, until lightning struck, so to speak.

Then, each day she set out from her townhouse on East Sixty-third Street to convince luxuriant kulaks that the museum's latest scheme to spend their money would somehow be like discovering a fortune under the floorboards of a rotting cabin they were about to sell to developers. She imparted to them that she alone had given them leave to make taste, and they were profoundly grateful to her for parking their ill-gotten gains.

She has an eye for the perfect architecture of the instant—once Nuala heard herself say that of Artemisia, their bond was indissoluble, because a person of such measured response is as valuable as the Rosetta Stone, and Nuala never cast off her valuables. All that had been left for her to do was to freeze-dry their bond with her rage. (It might be said in her behalf that she would have thought it funny if she'd known that when her husband, Joe Feeney, finally heard about her rage toward Artemisia, he thought it made her look like an evil rabbit.)

I've not only restretched and cleaned the gods all these years, I've managed to conjure them, she told herself. They owed me and they've struck the bitch down in the prime of life, just like that, turned her into a pot of ash.

24

Her curse on Artemisia Cavelli had picked the treacherous twat out of a thousand trees and shrubs and creepies and crawlies and fried her like bacon on a mountaintop. Nobody deserved it more. But it was a bit operatic.

Joe, always the Argus-eyed publicist, habitually lost control of his watery blues at the sight of a pair of well-turned legs, but Cavelli owed Nuala a little gratitude for all Nuala had done for her. Cavelli could have refrained from boffing Joe. And what made it even harder to stomach was Cavelli's well-known sexual ambivalence, although, come to think of it, Nuala wasn't sure how well known it was to anybody but her.

Nuala had put Artemisia's paintings in her now famous *Twenty Americans* show when Artemisia was only twenty-four. She'd invited her to the most prized soirées, she'd even taken her on a European speaking tour. She'd introduced her to the critics who count, the ones who find the smell of money aphrodisiac. She'd led Artemisia by the hand into the magic circle of aficionados whose love of themselves imbues the art they embrace with a sheen that can't be conveyed to the public even by the cleverest wall plaques. Joe and Artemisia basked in the light Nuala Gwilt shed, and so it was only natural, to her way of thinking, that they should pay her back by indulging a shabby little affair. After all, no one wants to think they owe all to a single person, especially not one as inevitable as Nuala. Oh, she understood their tawdriness very well. She didn't need Artemisia, so having her struck down by lightning was predictable, but Joe still had his uses. He was presentable, supportive, a born errand boy.

It would have been more pleasant had the girl been poor. Nuala was annoyed to have benefited from Artemisia's wealth. The memory of it diluted the quality of her revenge.

Whereas Renaissance paintings of gods and goddesses had always struck her as bourgeois, she now regarded them on her daily rounds with a wary eye. She'd taken good care of them, restraining overly aggressive conservators, and now the gods— one of them at least—had rewarded her. It didn't matter which one, but if she had to guess she'd say Pan. None of her minimalist

25

or postmodern paintings could have done the same. There's no use praying to a Motherwell to strike down a tart, and curses are merely lost in the tubular rhymes of a Jackson Pollock, although Motherwell might have drowned the cunt in a dozen degrees of darkness. Yes, that's a curse for another day.

Coming to a blushing Rubens lactation she had a vision of Joe furiously flubbing his underpowered contraption in front of photographs of the naked Artemisia Cavelli. They would have been the work of Henson Flyte, who'd vacationed with them on Martha's Vineyard. She shuddered with disgust at the thought of their idyll having provided Joe with pornography. Because she'd killed the girl she would henceforth have to think of any image of her, whether risen in the mind or laid out on a table, as pornography.

"Damn it, dead is dead," Nuala said.

"I'm sorry, Ms. Gwilt, I didn't hear you . . . ?"

"Oh, it's nothing, I'm just making a mental note of something."

Thinking about Artemisia and Joe reminded her of leaving a particularly sordid budget meeting with the museum board a few years ago, standing outside in a noisy rain, raising her arm to hail a cab and puking out into the street. She wanted to puke every time she looked at Joe. She'd arrange for him to get his, but not yet. It needed to be a thousand cuts to make up for Artemisia's Wagnerian exit. Offing Artemisia was just too merciful, too grand. She would have preferred whipping the girl for months on end, plucking her hair with pliers, hooking her up to batteries. Women were worthy of such considerations. What are men worthy of? What are they good for? Screwing up, making a hash of things. I was kind to her to the end, letting her die on the top of a mountain in the melodramatic Catskills.

Some classical god or goddess threw that bolt at Cavelli, no doubt, and one of these fine mornings before the hoi polloi contaminate the sanctuary, that deity will wink and have a little snigger. Meanwhile Nuala gave thanks every morning while flossing her teeth. It was only prudent to do that, even if she would have wished a more exquisite death for Artemisia.

26

Putting up with Joe Feeney in bed was like sacrificing to the gods. It was for a greater good, although it was hard to keep that greater good in mind. Not that he was an inconsiderate or unskilled lover, he was not, but everything he said sounded like flackery. He tasted like white peach. His hands were beautiful but not, like Artemisia's, capable. His hair was fine and smelled like strawberries. But his words might as well have been farts, and Nuala needed words to stir her syrupy blood, except where Artemisia had been concerned. She'd never found a single nuance of the bitch's body that didn't quicken her. She could have made a career of studying her, so subtle the signals she emitted, so coded the signals she elicited. And yet Artemisia spoke that language perfectly, a tongue Nuala could only guess at. The girl had been in every sense Florentine.

Nuala had never been jealous of anyone in her life. She'd been too busy. But now she imagined all the rooms where Artemisia had spoken her fey language with other girls and other women, and she feared she'd go on imagining it for the rest of her life, and it would steal the élan she needed to operate in her heady domain. And what aggravated her even more was that she knew that she, the girl's benefactress, hadn't known her erstwhile protégé at all. No, Artemisia's body had been fragrant with secrets, secrets with which she was born. Her clothes teased you with them. Only old Botticelli would have understood this. Her eyes pitied you for your ignorance of them. But they never pitied you for being you.

Nuala wept.

So when she thought about it, which was half-hourly, why did that bitch let Joe Feeney into her mysterium? It certainly wasn't an allure that she, Nuala, overlooked in him. No, it must have been simply to avenge herself on Nuala. But for what? For Nuala's power? For her generosity? Was it just to have a good laugh on somebody who took herself entirely too seriously? That notion stuck in her craw. And yet Artemisia never seemed to her a person moved to have a laugh on anybody. She'd have to give her that. She even tolerated pomposity, and was in fact amused.

She thought of whipping Artemisia. She thought of the cruelest whips. The thought was lubricious without being pleasant, like a slow, chill, painful climax. She'd have to settle for pissing on Artemisia's grave. Make a note. Where is she buried? Did they incinerate her? They probably wouldn't have been able to have an open-coffin funeral. She'd never met any of Artemisia's relatives. Who had buried her or laid her ashes? Did she have a will? Was there any family left? Had anyone ever done a portrait of her, of those disturbing gray eyes? She was startled at how little she knew about her victim.

Wouldn't it have been exciting to beat the girl repeatedly and then go about each morning acting as if nothing happened? Isn't that what they'd done to her, act as if nothing had happened? It's true we must be careful what we wish. It had been a fine curse, even if it hadn't captivated the gods, but it hadn't reflected what she really felt. She'd destroyed a nakedness she longed for and would go on longing for. That wasn't very clever, was it, Nuala?

She wondered, not just now but every day, how she would have felt, what sort of person she would be, if she'd been discovered by her own parents. She wondered why they hadn't prevented her, how she'd slipped through the cosmic sieve, and when she considered the improbabilities, of which she was the chief, it moved her, compelled her to discover artists and to conduct herself toward them as if she knew she'd discovered them, rather than conveying to them, as so many curators do, that by great good luck they'd been included in a show.

If you were Nuala's discovery, you enjoyed it. You knew that the heavens had noticed. You'd become important, even when she introduced you to the gods. They were lucky to meet you. She took your calls, sent you notes, called you darling and kissed you warmly even when there was no one else to notice. It never felt like luck. It felt like your just desert.

Of all the things for which she understandably gave herself credit, this wasn't one of them. It escaped her. It flowed in a pure dark understream from her experience of Isolde and Cleary Gwilt, whose perfect home had no affect, no warmth, no endearing flaw. She looked and looked at Isolde and Cleary and saw nothing but their inoffensive features. She couldn't remember their ever looking at her. When they were gone— killed as their airliner fell while taking off in Trieste—she found no photos, not of them or their child. They had gazed out upon their calamitous century with Etruscan and Greek eyes, raising her by the books, studying her as a wondrous creature somehow not their own, avoiding her eyes, indeed her creatureliness. I was their treasured disconnect, Nuala told friends, their equity in a world they really didn't want any part of. The result, of course, was that to Nuala's mind a bill of divorcement is implied in all relationships, but it would be tacky to dwell on it, in the way lawyers are tacky. It's just a compact between civilized people, like not asking personal questions.

Hendryck Lycoming, her predecessor and mentor, warned her about people like Cavelli. Your gifts to them will tyrannize you, he said. Be dispassionate, Nuala, cold if you will, because your enthusiasms will be turned against you. Whoever needs something from you, that's your enemy, Nuala. You must never let them become more than an ephemeral installation.

One white rose, I must go and put one white rose on your grave, Hendryck.

His cynical advice had been a grand gesture from a giant to his chosen successor.

Nuala's was a military power. It depended on knowing how the enemy thinks and what he wants. In her world knowing the enemy was always entrée. When she'd studied art history at Sarah Lawrence she didn't want to be an art historian, she wanted to be indispensable, like Rasputin. Not an authority but one who defined authority. Harold Rosenberg and Clement Greenberg could have the notoriety, the adulation. Nuala would have Midas's ear. The critics would be her lackeys, however much they mugged artists. Military intelligence isn't about what the enemy does, it's about his thought patterns. The Germans knew the Allies would land at Pas de Calais because that's what they themselves would do, what any logical enemy would do, and that's why the Allies landed at Normandy. The rich want to know what will make them richer, but they also want to look as if they've been rich a thousand years. They understand all about figureheads. You have to have generals who look like generals, CEOs, museum directors. If they do too much thinking on their own, well, that's one of the annoyances of real power. Lycoming looked as if he'd forgotten more than anybody else had ever known. Nuala looked as if you had the good taste to know her. If you happen to know what you're doing, that's a plus, but above all you must seem as if the powers that be know what they're doing. Joe was, of course, the perfect husband to savor this, since he made a living shaping appearances. That he had an exciting inner life no one knew or cared. He himself often thought of John Clare's heartbreaking line, *I am; yet what I am none cares or knows.*

We catch each other's attention in ways that are hard to film, ways hard for the eye, for all its acuity, to apprehend. Each of us has a language. When the Greeks said Athena whispered to people in their own tongues, they may well have meant this. It was the hush about Nuala that drew Joe, the sense she gave that words harm the matter at hand. Things slowed down and took up orbit around her. She was a reticent oracle. Small, furtive shadows caressed her alabaster cheeks, calves, and arms. But it wasn't Joe's flighty red hair or paradoxically still gaze that arrested her. It was their opening conversation at a Mary Boone Gallery reception. Joe was standing in front of an immense minimalist painting in which all the action and sensibility thrived in the cracks between big psychotic blocks of unctuous color, his thin body perfectly still.

"It won't get any better with time, you know," she said.

She ran an impeccably manicured forefinger around the rim of her champagne flute, as if trying to make it sing.

Joe's eyes slid over to her before he turned to search her face. The habitual readiness of his regard to entertain any notion tricked more silliness out of her.

"One might think the artist had paid you to stand there in such reverence," she said.

His lower lip hardened. This wasn't going to be somebody he'd like.

"I think we have a case of mistaken identity here. I'm not the person you're talking to."

It would have been perfect drawing-room British if only he'd said to whom you're speaking. He looked over Nuala's head and headed for the buffet. She then and there decided she had to know Joe Feeney, and although she was disappointed when she learned his name—she wanted something tonier—his response occupied its own shelf in her mind. Ignorance sometimes gets off with being arch, and either Joe knew who she was and didn't want to be toyed with or he'd simply blown her off as a gallery twit, which she'd momentarily been. Nuala knew that to make what you say count you have to count your words. She was upset that she'd said something so vapid, something she didn't even believe, and she'd been upset ever since that their relationship had cowed the Joseph Feeney she met that night.

The savvy that served him so well at that moment fell to pieces when she charmed him with a note three days later saying that a critic or curator with a closed mind is a mockery and she'd like to know why the artist Maxim Cruz had had Joe's rapt attention that evening at Boone's. Poor Joe, he still didn't know Nuala Gwilt was the gatekeeper de rigueur. He responded to her note out of ordinary politeness. A Cruz painting, he wrote, was like seeing an old lover for the first time.

Oh for Chrissake, she'd thought, you can't say things like that and have a name like Joe Feeney.

Their first encounter set the tone. She made a living, prestigious if not lucrative, wresting the right words from stone moments, but her word-craft struck Joe as pretentious. He knew a thing or two about words.

First he invited her to The Carlyle cabaret, a stylish but not insightful move. In time they came to enjoy long walks together. They found that, in spite of first impressions, neither of them valued repartée as much as unguarded observation. Day by day, often during lunchtimes, Joe discovered Nuala's secrets. He had room for them, having so few of his own. But, as she had failed to see the worlds in the cracks of Maxim Cruz's huge canvases, so she failed for many months to find in Joe the wonders that instantly delighted children and magi. She noticed that children, dogs and vagrants were drawn to him. He learned that she was famous, wrote for hoity-toity reviews and catalogues raisonnés. But only after they'd become diffident lovers—more like brushing against each other—did she recognize that there wasn't a block of Manhattan on which he hadn't found beauty—a face, festoon, cornice, corbel, iron grille, something etched into wet cement. There wasn't a day in which he hadn't overheard a conversation that enchanted him, nor a day when he hadn't recited a Yeats poem to himself.

What troubled Nuala about this slowness to appreciate a man she was already bedding was that she knew she was herself just the sort of person one imagined enjoying such small wonders, but she wasn't that sort of person at all. Hendryck Lycoming had lived for the privilege of every day discovering some small detail in a painting. Nuala was, like her writing, inclined to be granted unjust credit. She treated Joe in the high vaults of her mind as if he were a cranky, head-butting goat, whereas the man was a gazelle.

And when Nuala Gwilt discovered Artemisia Cavelli and began inviting her to receptions and hanging the girl's work in authoritative shows, Joe thought he'd developed asthma, because he couldn't breathe in Artemisia's presence, and when she drew close to him he began to topple towards her. It was like removing someone's mask at a ball and seeing yourself, the person you'd disguised. They'd stand in front of a painting and she'd point with her pinky, which he knew she used to scrape and rake paints, to just the thing that interested him, or she'd pluck the thoughts from his head while he was weighing their consequences. He knew about her, almost from the start, what no one else knew: Artemisia wasn't really human. She was faking it. And she knew he knew. He was Nuala's vassal but Artemisia's conspirator.

There's something about being lovers that nulls the best in each other. What escapes Joe is that Nuala is a connoisseur of the precariousness of everything. Only that distinguishes her as a curator. If he saw that, he'd understand that the sexual stasis between the three of them had been not only acceptable to Nuala, it was delectable. And inviolable. Nuala lives in the viral air. That's real enough for her. The worse she could say of a work of art is it's overdone, as most art is. Hers is the perfect sensibility for an art world power broker: the pooh-bahs she moves must think it their idea to be moved, and so nothing is forced into being, nothing is ever allowed to shuffle from the exquisitely possible to the obvious. No hint is ever made a nudge.

It's probably inevitable that a man who designs sales campaigns for banks and investment houses, a man who puts a smiling face on greed, will try, like some Cagliostro, to animate the frieze in which their lives are set. A man who finds something ineffably precious on every block of human consciousness shouldn't be doing what Joe does for a living.

It was okay for the three of them to swim naked in Domenico di Mongliano's moonlit Carrara marble pool, okay for Artemisia, topless in underpants, to paint Nuala nude on a hot Vineyard day and for Joe to serve them lemonade, but forbidden to presume these intimacies had consequences. Joe is accustomed to disguising piracy, and much as his refinement favors him with delicacies like those Vineyard days, it can't prevent him from leaving them just as they are.

Nuala savored the scents of their imaginations. Only barbarians would press for more. More would be overwrought, crass. Some things can exist only in their original settings, like ice sculpture. She regards exciting relationships as a kind of psychic frottage. The idea of fulfillment strikes her as gross. Joe will mourn the loss of this elegant idea for the rest of his life. Death will be anticlimactic. Everything that drew him to Nuala Gwilt is bound up in this idea.

What if no one ever smiles at me from a bus again? I might lose the chance to tell a stranger that all I wanted from Nuala was a midnight ferry ride to an island where we're brother and sister, where we realize we don't need anyone else, where for all our imaginings we can't imagine anyone tasting better, can't imagine anyone else's humors or . . . growing up. What if an old man who looks like God never nods at me again? I'll lose the chance to tell Nuala I regret the loss of our lives before Artemisia. One thing hinges on another. The smallest thing foretells a great event. A stranger's glance is often a secret license to turn inside out a life the stranger will never see. Joe's sense of connectedness is like a continuous rebirth. He's always having to grow up in the instant.

This is what Joe wants from strangers, to tell them that the precarious thing he'd wanted from Nuala has come and gone before he knew it, and he's become as unremarkable and as essential as a linchpin. Without his consent, without his knowledge even. He wants from strangers permission to keep on living as diligently as he's tried to live until now. But he also wants, perhaps all of us do, permission to do the unthinkable.

When he met Nuala and started walking around Manhattan Island with her he studied her not as a prospective sister with whom he might have sex but as a sister with whom he'd had sex from the start, even before they knew how to have it. In that way the mating game was mercifully set aside. He'd studied her as the inevitable sexual partner, not because she'd been convenient, but because he couldn't comprehend sexuality without remembering the moment his sister's legs looked not just like legs but suggestions, couldn't comprehend sexuality without remembering Marjorie scampering up a tree ahead of him, without remembering her unguarded scent, without remembering a dual sexuality meant to complement his own.

In fact, when he introduced Nuala to Marjorie, his sister had looked at him as if they were both falling in a torn hot-air balloon.

It follows that he should appreciate Nuala's love of the forbidden and the unfulfilled, but for that very reason he doesn't. And he doesn't guess how much it would have refreshed their friendship if he'd told Nuala about following Marjorie up a tree, if he'd managed to convey how much of his libido remained lost in the branches of that tree. Nuala lives for such glimpses into our hidden selves. But she has no idea how easily they make us murderers.

In the world the real Joseph Feeney lives in, we wordlessly know each other's take on things. Not the authorized versions we dry-clean for effect, but the unexpurgated realities we know would get us locked up. In this world, Feeney World, people dare to be nice to each other without fearing third-party responses. He calls this world Maloo.

It was Marjorie who unwittingly opened the door to Maloo. Terry, who belonged to the last generation familiar with it, taught her daughter the simple game of stealing partners called *Skip to My Lou*. Hand in hand, couples skip around a lone boy. *Lost my partner, what'll I do,* they sing. He hesitates and turns, trying to decide which girl to choose, and he sings, *I'll get another one prettier than you.* When he finally grasps the hand of the girl he has chosen, her partner takes his place in the center of the ring.

This was the game into which Marjorie dragooned her brother day after day. *Loo, loo, skip to my Lou, my darling.* But Joe heard it as Maloo, a magical place to which he just might someday skip. That's the way filmmakers heard it in 1931 when they made *Skip the Maloo.* Joe knew Marjorie always had a specific girl in mind and he took great pains not to choose that one, but he was never sure he'd thwarted her designs.

His take, which wasn't part of the game at all—it usually wasn't with him—was that if he jumped high into the air in the center of the ring he'd be transported to Maloo and there a magnificent caliph would take a liking to him and give him magical powers. Then he'd return home with these secret powers, and he would be very kind and make all his loved ones and friends rich and happy.

Years later, searching the Internet for ideas with which to disguise his banker-clients' avarice, he found a number of places called Maloo, one of them in New Zealand, as well as Maloo families in India, Pakistan, England and France.

He learned that loo is the Scots word for love, and he even found a theory that Lou derives from *lieu*, the French word for place. None of this diminished one bit the magical kingdom of Maloo from which his real friends and loved ones looked down with compassion on his mission in Manhattan, which he could never quite get straight.

Some day perhaps he'd tell somebody about Maloo, which was prospering in his head every day, but he didn't think anything bad would happen if he died not having shared Maloo. And only occasionally he encountered anyone whose own Maloo he badly wanted to visit. Artemisia excepted. She obviously lives in Maloo, albeit not Feeney Maloo.

Joe has no idea whether Nuala and Artemisia were lovers. But he loves knowing how much turned on his not knowing. Henson Flyte's camera thought they were lovers. But cameras lie, one reason we suffer such dreadful leaders. In the end Flyte's camera broke the spell. Neither their personal beauty nor the beauty of their friendship survived being photographed.

When Joe looked at Nuala he saw diamonds, obsidian, rubies, opals—an adytum whose masked adepts could not in their hearts say for certain whom their mistress served. That money is attracted to the possibility of more was the premise of his own career, but he saw that what attracted money to Nuala was the prospect of spending it unforgettably.

When he looked at Artemisia, who grew up rich and studied in Paris, Florence and Venice, he saw the teeming, unknowable sea, yet, always available, the sine qua non of life. Nuala existed to find her, and for this she deserved everlasting fealty.

What did he deserve? He didn't know, so he enjoyed the unaccountable privilege of being there.

But who could know any of this about Joseph Aloysius Feeney from Hauppauge, Long Island, and Fordham U? Who could know people were poems in his head? He'd easily become one of those inevitable New Yorkers who slip anonymously through office politics and mergers and investigations, who drink companionably but not heroically, who vanish grinning on weekends and return like triumphant quarterbacks on Monday, not too popular for his own good but too popular for his own comfort.

Nuala's best installation was their friendship with Artemisia. It could be seen from any angle. It had no back or front or side. It needed no special lighting and enjoyed the dark. It was Nuala's single work of art, and the only thing she asked of Joe and Artemisia was that they not spoil it. In return she was prepared to shower them with gifts, Artemisia with acclaim and Joe with esteem, elegance and glorious vacations. It was either a small or an impossible favor to ask.

Nuala once stunned a London conclave of art historians by calling Velasquez's celebrated Rokeby Venus glib. At the reception after her talk, Artemisia, whom she'd taken on tour with her, was asked about Nuala's remark. Nuala was out of earshot, but Artemisia's response got back to her:

"I do think the parts more interesting than the whole."

What a wonderful girl I've chosen for myself, Nuala had thought.

And that was perhaps the problem. She'd chosen Artemisia for herself, not for Joe or anyone else, and no one can survive such a choice, ever.

As for Artemisia's artful support of Nuala's cantankerous remark, it was candid. She loved the shadows and catenaries Velasquez gave Venus, but she found his masterpiece cloying.

The air conditioner is broken the day Nuala first meets Artemisia at Pratt Institute in Brooklyn. She's there to lecture about the postmodern period. She despises the subject in spite of being thought its owner. She understands little about it and believes she shares that in common with everyone else, which is why sycophants are happy to make her its arbiter. She's an acknowledged scholar, recognition being cheap in a time of insatiable hunger for trivia. Once the girl, then only nineteen and on her late summer break from Yale, floats up to the lectern to speak with her after the lecture, Nuala can't take her eyes off those nipples as they hip-hop under an Albini silk shirt. The alternative is to drown in those North Sea eyes.

Dripping with perspiration and dying for a cool drink, she stands there like a schoolgirl, desperate to detain this creature. She reminds herself she's famous and important and the girl is buttering her up, but she knows better from the start. This one wouldn't butter anyone up. Anybody could see that. She simply wants to talk about the lecture. What can she say to rivet this strangeling?

"It was a stupid lecture, Miss, I'm sorry, I didn't get your name."

"Cavelli, Artemisia Cavelli."

"What a lovely name. You have a famous namesake."

"Gentileschi, yes, my father wanted me to think about her. I had the sense, Ms. Gwilt, that you don't understand postmodernism any better than the rest of the critics."

This is practically license to admire the girl's nipples. Such a bold insult, and so right. If you're insulted you can stare.

"Well, I'm a curator, Ms. Cavelli, so I should know a little more than the critics, don't you think?"

"I think most of us hone our skills at acting as if we know more than we do. That's the easiest way to impress instructors and peers. It has to do with their insecurities."

My God, what a job it would be loving this creature. How tall is she? Five-eleven, at least.

"Do you have some work to show me?"

I never ask anybody to show me work. They're liable to do it. Especially not a nineteen-year-old student. But I'd like to get near enough to smell Primavera here.

When Artemisia produces her sketchpad she doesn't leaf through it looking for candidates to show Nuala, she simply hands it to her. The fragrance from the cleft of that small, high bosom intoxicates Nuala. Nuala wonders how she can make her examination of the sketches desultory but not hurtful. And then she sees the nude. Her nervous fingers stop. She looks up into her image in Artemisia's pupils.

"My grandmother. We posed for each other. She drew well, but she didn't paint."

"This—" (Nuala hopes the girl will take the tears forming in her eyes as sweat), "this could be a Parmigianino. You know him?"

"Yes, he didn't paint very much, but he drew like an angel."

Nuala slowly turns the pages.

"May I have it?"

She holds up the entire book, not just the page with the nude. It's a preposterous request, one that's simply not made. The girl probably needs the sketches for a class.

"I'd like my grandmother back, otherwise please keep them."

That's the drawing Nuala wants, of Haley Pennock. But she'll never see it again. Artemisia correctly sees that Nuala recognizes it as a source of authority. It's talismanic. She requests it several times for exhibitions in the ensuing years, and Artemisia always says she'll have to find it. But they both know she knows exactly where it is, in her safekeeping. It's the drawing of an ageless source, a figure condescending to appear vaguely human only for the purposes of the moment.

May I have it? Bold question, bold result. They'll see each other again.

You were thinking on your feet, Nuala, as usual. So was the girl, but what was her game? Nuala no more knew now than she'd known then, but she knew it wasn't to use Nuala, to use a chance encounter to make her way in the world. No, that wasn't Artemisia's way. This girl would float and lope through life on some unfathomable mission.

I never did learn her way, Nuala mused, but if she hadn't betrayed me, I might have. She did know me, she did know I'm half brilliant and half con artist, and damned near everybody in my world is. Artemisia knew that and didn't like or dislike it. Some hip shrink said if you meet the Buddha on the road, kill him. What schmaltz, it's what we always do. We were meant to kill each other, but Artemisia got off with her mojo, that incredible chalk and charcoal drawing of her grandmother.

If Joe thought what he had to do was as simple as a man importuning the symmetry of two women in love he would have gladly become a eunuch or slipped away like a seal off a wet rock, but people harbor opinions about each other that can't be reconciled to the facts. Their opinions strike them as divine, whereas the facts quibble. And there's another problem. People move on from where we leave them. Their hearing changes. Their vision. Their affect. We can't go back to find them. They need to be hailed in some new way we can't find, and they're irked by the old ways. They're not there, where we left them, but we are, and we're alone, and all is lost, especially the occasion that never was and so becomes a myth.

Except for Artemisia. She moved on, yes, but left few behind. She started drawing a warding circle around Peter Vogel's secret life and closed it in their senior year by marrying him. From the day they arrived at Yale his pale wintry eyes looked at her as if she were the last person he would ever see, perhaps the last person he wanted to see. The stony institutionalism of the place bent his shoulders and bowed his head. A small pure light in him guttered in the drafts of prescribed exchange. Once they'd become friends Peter began to tell her strange things that resonated with her experiences.

"Did you know, Artemisia, you have a way of appearing out of nowhere when you're least expected? People bumble in crowds, but you part them like a dolphin. I spot you across a gymnasium and next thing I know you're standing next to me. I think you're a shapeshifter. Did you know, Artemisia, metallic eyes are associated with prophecy? Uh, and, and witchcraft. There was a gray-eyed family in Normandy with strange powers . . ."

As Peter spoke, leaves clawed along the path they were following, imparting to her a feeling of weightlessness, as if he'd mentioned her natural state. She did feel more often than not she could pass through barriers by some act of will she'd mislaid like a fond piece of jewelry. And the idea that Peter should have apprehended this convinced her: she cupped his small flame with her hand in exchange for his insight.

She clutched his arm and tugged him along.

"I don't seem to have ordinary problems getting from one place to another. Distance and time have never seemed particularly formidable."

Peter threw open his palms and smiled.

No matter they separated two years after graduation, she remained his wife and friend. She was the only person in the world who understood his profane love for his twin Delia.

Their story came to Artemisia like the fragrance of daffodils in spring. She saw Delia reading by the Women's Table fountain, one leg up, a foot on the ground. They'd never met, but they looked forward to each other's smiles. Artemisia took a book from her backpack and began reading. After a while Delia brushed Artemisia's bare arm with her hand. The gesture was so wistful that Artemisia was afraid to look up for fear Delia would think she'd trespassed. She read for a few minutes more and then she ran the fingers of her left hand through Delia's blowy flaxen hair.

And then she knew.

She got up and walked away with Delia and Peter in her care. They weren't meant to cope with things as they are. They'd come to Yale to find her. With her they needed no one, but alone in the world they were naked.

Because Artemisia was wealthy, even by the crypted standards of a place used to wealth, she was able to inveigle data from her advisor, Miriam Cohn. Delia and Peter Vogel, identical twins, came from near Red Deer, Alberta. Their father, Joachim, grew red wheat and was literally threshed to death in a freak combine accident. Their mother, Hanne, sold their land, with its mysterious crop circles, to send them to private school in Calgary and then to Yale. She died in their sophomore year, the autumn before Artemisia and Delia wordlessly met by the Women's Table.

"It's too much, Artemisia. Just too much. Don't even think it. Stay away."

"Think what?"

Miriam Cohn didn't like Artemisia. She envied her poise and money. But it made her a good counselor, because she strove decently against her base instincts to do her job. It was a challenge, one Artemisia appreciated. She wasn't that fond of Miriam, but Miriam was resourceful and savvy.

"I know what you're thinking, Artemisia."

"Yes, and maybe Hanne when she was dying prayed they'd meet someone like me at Yale. When you think about it, Miriam, it would have been a forlorn hope. We don't exactly thrive on pink intimacy in this gray place, do we? But I can't help thinking Hanne knew she'd be putting them into my care."

"Do you have any idea how batty you sound, Artemisia? What, just think about this, what would your mother say?"

"Fortunately I don't have to think about it. She'd think like you, or worse. But she was never important. She just gave birth to me. It's what my grandmother Haley would say, and Haley would say, Do what you must, Artemisia. And it's Haley's money I'd be doing it with, you see. So that's it. Thank you, Miriam."

"For what? It's madness. I don't even know what you intend to do, but I can tell you it's crazy."

"Yes, thank you, it is crazy. I understand that. I'm not afraid of crazy. Isn't that why you don't like me?"

"Oh, Artemisia, let's just be student and advisor, okay?"

"Sure, that's all we are. Thanks, Miriam."

You go to college, if it's a good college, to get rid of your dangerous certainties, to find out how much you don't know, and to learn how to learn. Artemisia, Delia and Peter did well at Yale because they'd had few certainties to begin with and because they adored the galactic idea of how much they didn't know. One of their certainties—happily one for which there was no test—was that they'd come to Yale to find each other.

When holidays came the twins had nowhere to go after their mother died. They studied all summer between their sophomore and junior years, following their enthusiasms. Peter was enthralled by the Normans and couldn't think of anything more splendid than spending his life lecturing about them. His slight stutter abated when he talked about them. Delia slipped silently into Artemisia's sphere and decided to learn how to conserve paintings. The three spent Thanksgiving of their junior year in Artemisia's apartment in Manhattan. Then, with Christmas commercialism rising, it came to the twins: they had no home.

"Let's go to Palermo," Artemisia said. "There's a small market town, it's called Misilmeri, in the Eleutero Valley about twelve miles south of Palermo, where the Normans fought a great battle with the Saracens. We'll study the Saracen influence on the Normans. I'll make hundreds of sketches. Peter, you take notes. Delia, you photograph like crazy. We'll go to Christmas mass in La Chiesa Madre. We'll do a paper for someone."

They formed a circle, their arms on each other's shoulders, like Ouled Nail tribeswomen in North Africa, and danced for the sheer joy of Artemisia's idea. They had the feeling that if there were still gods, the gods liked them.

Back at Yale that winter Delia stroked Artemisia's thigh in their biology course and whispered, *We're symbionts, Artemisia*. But Artemisia wasn't so sure she was different from Delia and Peter.

Nuala knew none of this, and Joe didn't know why Artemisia had chosen to tell him about the twins. She hadn't even asked him not to tell Nuala. She knew he wouldn't, and that was much more than his wife knew about him.

People who stumble on fragile cabals, like Artemisia's with the twins, imperil them at risk to themselves. You can get away with a lot of shit, including greed and murder, but the old gods will wake up and hound you for betraying people like Peter and Delia. Or Artemisia.

Perhaps the young Artemisia wove a cover story for herself as well as Peter and Delia. Perhaps she'd made a marriage of the three of them, foreshadowing her marriage to Nuala and Joe. Such thoughts could be entertained. But Joe didn't believe them. Artemisia simply protected the twins. That's all he believed.

It wasn't too great a subtlety for him. By no means. But he had to barge into Artemisia's life anyway, and there was no life he viewed as more sacrosanct. He didn't want her to need his information, to need anyone or anything. That left no room for him, and yet no look she'd ever given him said go away. What made her an otherling in his view, a demiurge, was that she didn't look at anyone that way. Everyone was welcome to be seen. Who knows someone like that? Who has ever known a person like that? Only when myth defined the world were there creatures like that. In that world, the old world, Artemis was a virgin huntress.

And something else imparted her otherness to Joe. He'd once seen an old restored racing yacht from the 1930s sailing in Long Island Sound, leaning as a quartering wind drove her seaward. He'd leaned over as he watched, feeling like the yacht herself. He felt himself groaning in the wind, driven by a divine power. He knew nothing about sailing. But he started reading, and when he learned that wind is an aspect of the sun he felt like a metaphysician. Watching Artemisia in the street, before she noticed being noticed, she reminded him of the great yacht, driving inexorably seaward. She seemed to sail on the wind.

Some people become our baggage. We wish an airline would lose them. Most of Joe's successful acquaintances knew how to jettison people. Some were nice about it, some not, but they were all incomprehensible to him, because he felt we're put in each other's way for a reason. If that were not true, nothing would make sense. He used to think this was a Catholic thing—in this view shutting people out was an icy Episcopalian trait, heretical even—but eventually his inability to understand it just felt like herpes. And when it came to Artemisia it didn't matter because she was the sort of person who'd never shut anyone out. It worried him about her. What kind of a life could she have had protecting the twins from such an early age? And yet her life seemed complete. Sparing a few moments now and then to worry about himself in a similar vein never occurred to him. He certainly didn't think Nuala or Artemisia worried that he made "loans" to childhood friends afflicted with failure to thrive. He took these people's calls and never thought them hangers-on or nuisances.

Nuala admired this trait. She even tried to imitate it. It was the reason Artemisia had told Joe about Delia and Peter.

There were many unforgivables in Nuala's life, but they were mostly committed by artists against their materials. Artists whose career strategies led them to hit on her amused her. She complimented them for their good taste and conveyed her regrets. She preferred to do the hitting, and since her taste and discretion were equally impeccable nobody gave much thought to where Nuala Gwilt slept. In fact, she wasn't the sort of woman people imagined sleeping anywhere. Artemisia wasn't as impervious to such speculation, but once you started imagining yourself in her bed, dimensions of space and time lost their shape and you found yourself wondering how to get back to where you'd been. This sensation was perhaps a modern version of the death of Actaeon, the Greek hunter Artemis caught watching her bathe and turned into a stag, who was then torn to pieces by his own hounds.

Yup, he told himself in recent days, that's me, Joseph Actaeon Feeney.

When Henson Flyte switched on the red light in his darkroom he understood this Artemis in Artemisia. You might catch a goddess unawares, she might beckon you, but you'd lose everything and everyone you held dear. The next time he saw her in person his face twitched and he blinked too much. She smiled and ran her fingers down his face to restore its composure. She knew what he'd seen.

"Just give the photos to Nuala, Henson. Tell her you don't want to be associated with them. They don't meet your standards. She'll understand."

That's where it should have ended. But Flyte did a damn-fool thing. He had them delivered to the house on Sixty-third Street with a note. Nuala was in Santa Fe and Joe did another damn-fool thing: he opened the envelope, read the note, and put the photos in his wall safe, which hid behind a priceless Arshile Gorky. Months later, talking on his cell phone, he fetched a document from the safe and failed to spin its lock, leaving the safe open. That very evening Nuala noticed the Gorky ajar. She meant to close the safe's door and spin the lock, but the door swung out and there in open view were the photos of Artemisia, arrayed like a deck of Tarot cards.

You could say it wasn't the accident of the safe being left open that caused the trouble, you could say it was rather the implosion of Nuala's sense of proportion, or you could say a parasite infected her imagination. You could say she was jealous. Artemisia belonged to her. Joe was just a Greek chorus of one. But none of these possibilities was exactly true. To keep these failed art works in a safe for one's self-gratification was sordid. For Artemisia to undress in front of him, yes, that was understandable. But to let him have these bloopers . . . Nuala's bright mind went haywire and couldn't right itself, no matter how hard she tried to understand.

She announced she was going to vacation in Amalfi to regain her perspective about her work. It wasn't untrue. It was now her work to calculate just how to destroy Artemisia's career, which she had launched. How would she plant the seeds of doubt about Artemisia's work? How would she explain her earlier enthusiasm for the girl's work? Who would she entrust with the poison? Which critical minds would she bend against Artemisia? How would she prompt The Waterman Gallery to drop Artemisia? A few weeks in Amalfi was just the ticket to refine this scheme. It needed economy. It needed to seem casual. But it needed an engine.

It took no more than three days steeping in the Neapolitan sun to cook up her curse on Artemisia. But she never dreamed that some god she'd hustled to apostates in a museum five days a week would strike the damned girl dead only two weeks after Nuala had returned to New York.

Success isn't as much will as timing. Some things are going to happen and you either align yourself with them or you fiddle with fooleries. Something bad was going to happen to Artemisia Cavelli when Nuala returned from Amalfi. What was important was how Nuala spent her time waiting for it. This issue defined itself the minute she got back to her desk.

Vacations are dangerous, not because of Mexican bandits or Somali pirates but because of treachery at home. Vacationers may be leaving their livelihoods behind for good these days. You never know what's going to happen while you're gone. When Nuala opened the blinds in her corner office at The Chance Worrell Museum Institute, light fell on a conflict brewing between her and the towering matron she called Modthryth, after the monster queen in *Beowulf.* Modthryth was the new chair of the museum's friends. Seven memos from her and three museum directors explained that they had concluded Nuala's efforts to define Postmodernism had simply baffled the public and diminished museum support. Attendance was falling and so was private and institutional support. The public had finally gotten Abstract Expressionism and Pop and Op and Magic Realism and all the other word contraptions the big thinkers nail together, but it didn't get Postmodernism. What the hell was it? Malaise, miasma, a broad failure of vision? We need a director who will engage the public, not depress and confuse it, the memos said. This is the age of the global positioning device, one snide director wrote.

Well, she knew damned well what this was about. Her legs. It was about her legs. Modthryth's high-flying husband, one of the directors, couldn't talk straight when he saw Nuala in heels. She understood the woman's plight intimately, it being in a way her own. Modthryth hadn't found any naked Nualas in her husband's safe, but circumstances put Nuala and Modthryth's husband together almost weekly, and he'd jump through fiery hoops to breathe Nuala's secondhand air.

She sat in the glow of the hidden lights in her green glass desk, drumming the pads of her fingers.

It's always going to be said that successful women slept with the right men. Some do. And a lot depends on how you define the right man. Nuala never slept with the philanthropists she cultivated. She never slept with anyone she merely desired. After all, we consumers want a great many people and things and usually do ill by them. Nuala slept with people who would memorialize the event by letting a little bit of her excellence seep into their lives, mostly women, but occasionally the surprising man like Joe. Yes, the rousing musculature of her dancer's calves on occasion became someone's desperation, but she knew her quietude haunted people and her sexuality wasn't addictive and so could be donated from time to time.

Modthryh's husband would rein in his berserking wife simply because he preferred wanting Nuala to having her. He preferred the idea of it. The fact would constitute a poor investment. He'd go on behaving as Nuala had expected Joe to behave, and maybe that's why there was money in his safe instead of photographs.

As for the board, you need tension on a board. There were shows in the works that would boost attendance past projections, and there were large bequeathals, tantamount to nuclear blackmail, which she hadn't even yet announced to the board.

As she sat in the late morning sunlight she fondled in memory her temperate life before she'd met Artemisia. The problem with knowing Artemisia was that Nuala couldn't imagine life before her. It drained away like gray water. Her life before Artemisia had been an antiseptic waiting room. A person who knows there are incomparable paintings is unlikely to be surprised to meet an incomparable person. The trouble with Artemisia was that from the moment Nuala spotted her at Pratt she became the only planet on which Nuala's species could exist, the only air she could breathe. Everything else was contrived. Artemisia was the only natural force in the world. And responsibility for the precarious balance of her relationship with Artemisia fell to Joe. He was supposed to conduct himself in a way that sustained it.

Someone could have told him it was much too high a price, even for a pleasurable life spent between a townhouse on the Upper East Side and a saltbox on Martha's Vineyard, punctuated by artsy trips to Europe. But nobody did tell him. Everybody thought they knew him and nobody did.

Perhaps because she knew what people wanted to hear and parceled it out tactically, Nuala heard what she wanted to hear when Genevieve Paulsen told her about Artemisia. She wanted to hear what she'd already heard so that she could have a second chance at responding to it, so that she could improve her response.

"Nuala, darling, it's unspeakable about that magical protégé of yours. I'm so dreadfully sorry."

"Artemisia Cavelli?"

"Mmm. How unlikely, hiking alone like that . . . Nuala! You haven't heard? Oh my God! She was struck by lightning. I'm so sorry."

Nuala rushed to the public restroom off the museum's lobby, tears wobbling in her eyes. But when she arrived at a mirror she wasn't sure what the tears were for, whom they were for. Artemisia dead? Nuala alone? You are alone, Nuala. Curious word. Me? Alone? Who heard my curses, who acted on them? We all deserve another chance to react to the most dread news, or to the best news. We deserve to hear it right. We deserve a proper memory, a well-crafted one.

She swiped her tears with a pinky and tasted them. They were like a daub of pricey caviar.

This is the taste of solitude, Nuala. Is that you, with such power? Yes, I'd cry if I were you and had such power. I'd tremble. And now what's left without Artemisia to love or hate? How will the days pass? Why would they pass? All power is absurd, of course. But this is a joke. You're no more than you were before you met her. You forgot that the one thing we always are is alone.

"Nuala, can I help, darling?"

Genevieve would strike Nuala's enemies on the board off her social list rather than let them do Nuala in, and that would be like having their passports lifted by Homeland Security. But then Nuala would be Genevieve's little slavey.

Nuala brushed past her and hid in a toilet stall. She sat and listened to her bowels. Is it what she wanted to hear? It's what she'd heard. She made no inquiries the first time she heard it, and she'd make none now. Artemisia dead, struck down by a bolt from the heavens. How often we say, Oh I wish I'd said this or done that, and here Nuala had been given and had taken the chance to greet news of Artemisia's death all over again, correctly.

Did that sound right? No, it didn't.

49

This wasn't a chance to respond like the friend she'd been. It was a chance to plumb the true depth of her despair.

"You must muck out all your stalls, Grace. People like Monkridge and Cavelli are second-raters. They aren't going to get you any museum points, you know. Oops, my directors' line is lighting up. Must run, Grace. Toodle-oo."

In this way Artemisia's dealer, Grace Waterman, learned she and Artemisia had fallen from grace. The critics were learning in similar ways. Her current show went unreviewed by the majors.

And it's how Nuala's lightning struck Joe, too.

"What's going on, Joe?"

Grace didn't greet him, she didn't offer him coffee. She just asked him to her gallery on Chelsea's Twenty-sixth Street and grilled him.

"Joe? What is Nuala thinking?"

He didn't know Grace well enough to tell her. It might make things worse. It would make them worse. He'd always been able to make the dour Grace Waterman laugh. She was too earnest, too honest for her own good. She was one of those people who look more approachable than they are.

"I've been so busy convincing people the banks aren't robbing them I've been kind of out of touch. I better have a talk with Nuala before she changes the locks."

Grace tried to laugh, but it was as lame as his response. She wasn't just looking at Artemisia's fall, she was looking at her own. Artemisia was young enough and rich enough to take a fall now and then, but staggering under forty-four thousand dollars a month in rent, Grace couldn't afford one. Not even a misstep.

"Joe, I'd be grateful for whatever you can do."

They stood studying the fright in each other's eyes. They'd never really thought much about each other, but now they looked ordinary decency in the eye.

He nodded and left.

It didn't take long to find out what was going on. Nuala was what she called a visualist. She couldn't fully comprehend what

50

she couldn't see. You could tell her something a thousand times and not get through unless she could see it. The same was true of her own contemplations. So when Joe found a single Henson Flyte of Artemisia under Nuala's lingerie in a dresser drawer he understood everything. She'd asked him to toss a black bra to her in the bathroom. His fingers touched something brittle under her underclothes. Nuala had pinned a naked Artemisia to the bottom of her drawer, pinned her through the eyes and buried her in underwear.

It felt like stomach flu. He shivered in the light from the bathroom. He felt pins in his own pupils. He thought of Saint Sebastian, shot full of arrows.

"Joe?"

He jerked Nuala's bra tight, like a garrote. He didn't throw it to her, as she'd asked. He handed it to her ritually, but for a second he wouldn't let it go, like a priest withholding the chalice for a second. She took it, lowered her towel and tucked it in at her waist. Then she put the bra on. A smile flitted across her mouth. With his thumb he scraped the wickedness off her lips. Otherwise he would have killed her. This was the Joe she'd met at Mary Boone's, returned after all these years.

She had vacated her face, and all its radiance couldn't light a path back to it. He understood that porcelain face to be a homing device in the service of her polished, empty masters. Money and acclaim came to that device and were rerouted, but she wasn't there, so killing her wouldn't have done any good. It was her nature not to be anywhere and therefore to loom as a possibility everywhere. But if Joe had ever laid this out to her—he'd do it like a man fidgeting with silverware— Nuala would have dismissed it out of hand. She would also have had to reassess their relationship, because she had no clue Joe indulged such surreal ideas. He could have withstood living with an uninhabited Dresden doll if her dismissals didn't remind him of the most difficult clients at Gossaert Nostrand. What he couldn't figure out was what she'd done with her name when she vacated that face. It didn't strike him as a suitable traveling companion, that name. It was an adhesive name, not one you could pull off and wear around your finger when you decided to stroll in astral gardens. It was a place name.

She slid past him to her vanity and began to color her face. He turned and stared. It didn't matter, because the micro-weathers of his face and the insights that lit his eyes had never interested her. Nuala the visualist had never been able to visualize him. He might as well have been a mirror. Nuala dwelled in a forest of mirrors.

Listening to her shuffle her deck of privacies he mused with rue that life with Nuala was not unlike Tarot. Usually he thought himself the Hanged Man, but now he thought he might like to replace that notorious card with a Man of Untimely Epiphanies, because he had many epiphanies, his life was about them, but he didn't have them at the right time. For example, one night a year or more into their marriage, as she rode him shuddering and grimacing, he asked, You okay? I'm doing my business, she'd said matter-of-factly.

The armored privacy of her remark—a report, really—excited him. But days later, walking into a blinding sun, it hit him: her business, not his. That's what Nuala did, her business, and you were either a help or hindrance. In the dazzling sunlight he'd smiled at the thought of helping Nuala do such particular business, but now, listening to her dress, it felt like exile. Nuala would go on doing her business, shuddering and grimacing, with or without handy helpers. It felt too much like his work, helping others achieve bitterly focused ends.

There's a certain kind of Irishman whose Irishness is bestowed on him by others—he can either wear its flummery, putting it down to being a hard guise to get rid of, or he can find something more suitable to wear, like the kind of gaze that says, *Hello, who are you? I'd really like to know.* Joe's kind of gaze, the one Nuala never noticed. She thought it was part of a blarney he noticeably lacked, which is to say she'd somehow met and married him without noticing him.

It amused him. It enabled him to ghost around her without explaining, except at four o'clock in the morning when his mind felt like a plaster cast crumbling on a sculptor's bench. He'd wake up and watch her sleep, the sleep of the damned, he called it.

If words were just so much flatware, useful for eating at each other's table, if you were a genuine visualist, as Nuala was, you'd naturally want to marry a ghost, if you had to marry anyone, that is, because anyone else would be invasive. And if you ever fell in love—Joe's definition of love was that sensation of falling towards someone that he felt around Artemisia—you'd find a changeling to love, someone who not only didn't get in your way but knew exactly how to get out of your way.

They hadn't fallen in love, Nuala and Joe, they'd embarked on a search for Artemisia. Someone to consider in the middle of the night. Someone to wander all the rooms of their unexplored heads. Someone to leave each room just as they enter, to turn each corner just as they near.

Someone to destroy, Joe thought as he stood watching Nuala finish dressing.

"Claudine, did I hear that little ole you are the assistant hospital administrator?

"I don't know, dear, did you?"

"You're full of surprises, Claudine. I thought you spent your days kowtowing to specialist this and surgeon that."

"We're the Sisters of Mercy, Artemisia, so naturally we wouldn't want doctors making any important decisions, would we? I mean, they're so full of themselves."

"And a bit hard of hearing, Sister."

"Yes, that too, and that's why I want you to mince words and be as much as possible the Artemisia Cavelli you were before you climbed up Giant Ledge, and—well, that's just what I don't want you to talk about, because you sound goofy. You can believe anything you want to believe, but I want to believe you're smart enough to keep quiet about it and not play into anybody's hands. Understood?"

"Jahvohl!"

"I mean it, Artemisia, you're flirtuing with the brink of being institutionalized. We don't want that. I have enough paperwork already. We definitely don't want that."

"Because you like me?"

"Because I like you. And because we don't know what's in the head of that husband of yours."

Redmond Hazard keeps asking Artemisia where she is. He needs to wash his dark blond hair. It smells like spoiled brisket. He's handsome, this Hazard, and tedious.

"I'll tell you where I am. Just this once. Then don't ask me again. I'm exactly where a rational person would be under the circumstances."

He's drunk on the sweetness of my breath, can you beat that? This means he lives a secret, hazardous life, true to his name. Just as he was deciding he doesn't like me he gets wasted on my breath. I know I have extraordinary breath. Always have. Something in my chemistry converts garlic, gorgonzola and anything else into mint delight. So dirty-hair Hazard is a goner. I'll just sigh all over him and tell him about Giant Ledge. Then he'll know where I am and he won't have to worry about my being here. On the one hand he might like to put me away where he can quaff my breath whenever he likes, but on the other hand his idealism is such that he thinks such a fragrance should be let loose on the world.

"Okay, just this once. I'm thirty-two-hundred feet up on Slide Mountain. There's three inches of snow disguising an ice slick on the ground, so I'm still wearing my instep crampons. The sun looks like a cooling ember, but I can still see the Esopus Valley. The wind bonsais the balsams up there, so the ledge looks like a Japanese stone garden. There's a hundred-and-eighty-foot drop off the ledge onto the forest. The plastic windows of my octagonal blue tent are blood-red. The wind is rising behind me and when I turn into it I see a snow squall. It looks like a whirling dervish, stepping from one rise to another. Night is dropping around it like a stone. Suddenly lightning cracks open the sky. Everything is bright silver, pink and shadows. It's beautiful. Suddenly lightning cracks the world open in two places. I bounce on my feet. Next thing I know I'm looking up into these huge violet Sumerian eyes and the first thing that occurs to me is that these eyes don't belong to a human. I can't tell you how happy I am about that. It feels like when you run a race and it dawns on you slowly that you won. It feels like coming home. But then they have to go and tell me those eyes belong to a ranger lady who happened to be up there checking out fools like me, and my head is on her lap and she's thinking I'm toast. So that's where I am, Doctor Hazard, up there on Slide Mountain thinking I'll never again have to think anything anticlimactic like this."

"This, Artemisia?"

"Yeah, hospitals, husbands, taxes, friends, enemies. You."

"You have enemies, Artemisia?"

"They're not formidable."

"But you know them? I mean you remember having them?"

"Before I became the toast of the Catskills, you mean?"

Doctor Hazard smiles a stitchy, worrisome smile. Artemisia grants him a little analgesic huff. He looks as if he's just received communion. She smiles a disconcertingly sisterly smile, that once-in-a-lifetime smile bestowed on a brother the moment his sister happens into the naughtiest closet in his head.

This is not what Sister Claudine wants her to do. Sister Claudine wants her to stay out of others' heads, to act as if she'd just gone through Hazelden and is as sober as she's ever been, not high on lightning, silver and shadows.

"You're behaving like a dry drunk, Artemisia."

"How does a dry drunk behave, Claudine?"

"Sister Claudine to you. A dry drunk behaves like the president of the United States. You know, talking tough, cooking up a war, digging a hole to China and pouring our money into it, lying like a rug, convincingly."

"You're comparing me to Alfred E. Neuman, Claudine?"

"I'm warning you not to invite misdiagnosis. I believe in Transubstantiation, so it's not a stretch for me to believe your story, Artemisia, but Redmond Hazard is one of those people who would lock you up for it, or maybe he'd do it just so you could keep on breathing on him, have you thought of that?"

Ah, so Sister Claudine has noticed my breath.

"Won't you miss it, too? My breath, I mean."

"I miss a lot of things, Artemisia."

Her patient wishes Claudine would never have to miss anything or anyone. In the corner of Artemisia's left eye a tear glimmers. Sister Claudine steals it with her forefinger.

"There will be a fine white scar about an inch and a half long starting right here and stopping here. A little cosmetic surgery will take care of it."

The young surgeon is holding a mirror to show her how the scar will slant down towards the outside of her left eyebrow, like lightning.

"I think it will give me a touch of character."

"That's hardly one of your deficiencies, Artemisia."

"Perhaps you don't know me as well as you think, Claudine."

"Sister Claudine to you."

"Well, I think I'll keep it."

She doesn't watch television that evening, nor does she read. She files through her mind for all the drawings and paintings she's made of Delia and Peter and never gotten their haunted eyes right. Eyes are hard to do, mouths even harder. She'd always gotten their mouths right. Thin, the upper lips penned gracefully over the straight lower lips. But their eyes were so pale that the blue in them seemed to collect in the outer canthuses and drain away as you looked at them. No matter how many times she's thinned the cadmium blue or resorted to pastel, she can't convey the paleness of their eyes or the fact that surroundings seem to disappear in them.

She's worried about them. But she doesn't yet realize that only the day before she didn't remember them. Somebody has told them about the accident. Where are they? They'd been down in the parking lot. They'd looked disturbed. Of course they are.

Have they gone back to their Brooklyn studio on Old Fulton in Dumbo? Are they in a motel here? She doesn't want to explain them to Claudine or anyone. Maybe now she's lightning's child she'll get their eyes right. It's important. If she doesn't do it, who will? They must be frightened.

When she finally sleeps, she dreams about a royal blue plastic envelope. Eight by four inches, sealed by some kind of stamp that says Eire. It doesn't seem to have gone through a postal service. It's handed to her, but she can't remember the body, only the hand. A woman's hand. She opens it and a piece of crackled newsprint about three feet long sails away from her left hand. Artemisia is left-handed. She sees Cyrillic, Greek, Gothic and modern English letters. She sees letters she doesn't recognize. Arabic equations. But no Arabic, Hebrew, Sanskrit or Asian characters. She understands nothing, but it all seems familiar. She dreams she falls asleep with the newsprint covering her belly.

Two blue holes in the dark wake her. She hears three short blasts from the Hudson. A ship backing off the cement plant. She knows such things. She knows what the white lights stacked over the wheelhouse of a tugboat mean. She knows how long the towlines are. Once a sound or sight catches her attention, she spends time in the library understanding it. Knowing arcane things she doesn't need to know finds its way into her art. As the two blue holes prize open the space around her she sends her mind casting for anybody who's ever understood how things get into her paintings. She remembered Delia once said Artemisia couldn't paint Delia's pubis because nobody would believe it was silver. That was pretty astute, Artemisia thought. It certainly wasn't golden or even tow-haired, but Artemisia got it right, and Delia had been disappointed.

"Next time I'll even get its fragrance."

Delia had blushed and gotten off her modeling stage and kissed Artemisia's forehead.

Nuala Gwilt knew that somewhere in Artemisia's work was her knowledge of the horns and lights and humors of the East River. Nuala apprehended such things.

How do I know Nuala knows these things? It's because she smiled when I told her the reason Artemisia Gentileschi's *Judith Beheading Holofernes* is great is because Judith is gleeful, and you have to know a lot about Artemisia Gentileschi to know why Judith is gleeful.

Today Dr. Redmond Hazard is consulting with his itty-bitty committee, as Claudine describes them. The more Artemisia levitates in the great blue stare filling her room the more she recognizes that Claudine is warning her. The blue drains from the room and returns to its owner's eyes. Artemisia sees the owner's white fur. It reminds her of Delia's pubis. The wolf looks solemnly at the door to the room. Artemisia dresses. She writes on her sketchpad, *Dearest Claudine, I miss you already. I'll be in touch. Tell your sisters not to worry. I'll do something nice for them. I'm a sister too. But, as you know, I must go now. Love, Artemisia.*

Then she and Thunder leave.

"Whatever I don't remember you have to tell me, Thunder. For all I know the two lobes of my brain aren't talking to each other. Can I paint? Can I drive? Where's Minerva?"

Artemisia calls her Lexus Minerva.

Thunder walks slightly ahead to her left.

"Are you a girl?"

Thunder glances at her expressionlessly.

"Of course you are. A woman, I mean. You're a woman. A female wolf? A she-wolf? But nobody's consort, right?"

The sliding doors of the emergency room whoosh open for them. Outside Thunder turns and shoves Artemisia's left knee with her paw.

"I think Minerva's in the parking area at the foot of Slide Mountain, Thunder. Yes, that's where I left her. We'll have to get a cab. It's about an hour from here."

Gudrun Kierstadt, only a few days later, is accompanied by another kind of familiar, a nineteen-year-old Arab queen named Zenobia who is briefing her for the world of Fifth Avenue djinn.

You can live with someone you don't like for a long time, maybe the rest of your life, Gudrun muses. It feels like infidelity, only better. You're cheating on yourself and making up cover stories. They're all bullshit, like the one you tell the guy you don't like, the guy sleeping next to you: Would I still be here if I didn't love you? Of course you would. But he's stupid enough to believe you, which is how you know you really picked a winner. Loving somebody is easy, liking them is not, and therein is the saddest part of being human, that we don't hear ourselves over the din of our opera.

Usually the voices in your head are hollowed out, unless you lend them a little timbre and a bit of color. But then you'd be play-acting and they'd lose their innocence, the thing that makes you believe them. Of course you often manage not to believe them, which is why you're sitting here at four o'clock in the morning listening to Shithead snore. God, it's fun to call him names like that and watch him imitate a tolerant man. He's as phony as you are, maybe even more of a coward.

But the trouble is this particular voice, how would you describe it? It's not yours. It's not a voice you've ever had, even when you were capable of whispering a few silky lies in someone's ear. See if you can dump your crock of lies on the floor and listen. Maybe there's still somebody in the world worth listening to, besides Zvonko the Doorman.

There's a clique of djinn across the street in Central Park. You can see them best when it's snowing. Big top-lofty guys wearing head knots and regal robes knocking themselves out dancing and somersaulting. Their breaths are incredibly sweet. You can smell them right through the walls. This is the best time to see them. They don't mind the traffic, but they're aware that a few of us over here in our counting houses are listening to them, watching them. During the day they mimic snooty girls. They hoot at the leopard-coated dame of a certain age skiing on the pavement with her leopard-coated schnauzer and they mock-weigh in their hands the boobs of running girls. Altogether a louche bunch, I'd say.

59

So, djinn, what do you think of W. Eames Shithead here? What do you think of my new voice? What do you think of anything?

The one who sits on the Metropolitan Museum all day contemplating midgets heaves a huge sigh that steams her windows. An image from one of the Arab poets of al-Andalus comes to her: the river looks like a white hand parting a green robe. He's a djinni, so of course he knows from Arabs. But that's what this voice sounds like, and Gudrun knows she's never sounded like that, not in this life.

She turns around and regards Shithead. When his sinuses drain into his bilges and he's dressed and shaved he looks rather distinguished, as if he belongs in a boardroom in some capacity other than bringing in the drinks. When Shithead speaks the insiders listen. There are even some pretty classy chicks down there on Wall Street who think him worth distracting.

Don't you think it's time to let Shithead have a life? After all, he's never given you anything but money. What's the beef? Give him a break.

Is that you, the white hand opening the green robe? Is that you making the case for Mr. Shithead?

Don't you think he's entitled to a good lay before he croaks? Who knows, with a little luck one of those chickies might even like him. God knows, you don't.

What am I entitled to? Can you answer me that? Or am I supposed to be Mrs. Beneficence?

Dear, dear Mrs. Beneficence, yes, that's exactly who you are to be. Just get dressed and leave Mr. Shithead to the chickies, to the suck-ups. Leave him right there on those silken sheets and come with me.

You? And where are you going, Zenobia?

Well, Mrs. Beneficence, we're not going to have our nails buffed. We're not going to torment delivery boys. We're not going to get our asses polished by yet another curator who wants yet another donation for yet another painting. No, we're going to wear something decent and go find that zany girl we talked to the other day at the bandshell. The one who had a big fever and wound up in some hospital upstate convinced she had the mind of a long-dead Cathar who'd been a helluva lot smarter than her? Yes, that's the one. The twenty-something with the mind of an eighty-something, the one with the pale trancey eyes.

Ummm, yes, great legs, almost as good as mine.

Better, I think, if we're going to be precise.

Are we? Going to be precise?

Very.

Well, in that case, Zenobia, you'll recall she didn't say anything about being a Cathar. She didn't have time to tell me anything, really. We got pushed around by the crowd. But she had a white wolf that nobody saw, except us.

That's important, Gudrun. Now leave Shithead a note. No. That won't do. He never reads notes. They just confuse him. His mind is made up. He'll know exactly what to tell the police. They'll think he's a great guy.

He's not a bad guy, you know. I don't hate him.

You just don't like him.

He's really been very nice. He even agreed not to trouble himself with children. He'd have been a great father. We'd have bought a place in the Hamptons or in Dutchess, or both.

That's enough of that, Gudrun. It was a great mercy to the unborn, I think we're agreed about that.

Shouldn't we wait till the banks open?

You can wait till the voters smarten up, it won't make the slightest difference. That girl is waiting for us.

At four in the morning? Waiting for what? Are we going to be lovers? That's not a bad idea, you know. I could live with that. I did have the distinct feeling she'd taste very good. I haven't had that feeling in a long time.

She does taste very good, I assure you, Gudrun. But you're wasting your time. And mine. Maybe some Cathar has time to educate that girl, but I don't have the same kind of time to deal with you.

Oh, excuse me, your highness, I know your duty calls, so perhaps you might turn me over to one your courtiers, a handsome one with lots of money.

You've been there, done that, Gudrun. Shithead here is rich and still handsome in a ripe sort of way. A foxy sort of way, I should have thought.

Gudrun was seven when she met Zenobia. Then and now, Zenobia was nineteen, imparting to her as much wisdom as Gudrun could take, usually comforting but sometimes frightening her. In the fright Zenobia came alive. Other times Gudrun feared she'd invented her, and yet Zenobia's voice never changed. If her vocabulary had grown it merely kept up with what Gudrun could understand. Its tone remained measured, humorous and profane. In the forty years they'd known each other Gudrun made the decisions and Zenobia guided her through their consequences, one of them being Shithead here. This arrangement always struck Gudrun as ideal. But Zenobia was still a nineteen-year-old Arab queen, while Gudrun was a sore-footed do-gooder, miserable about betraying a gift that frightened her, married to a celebrated boor, and bent on dumping a high-handed museum director.

What should I have done with this gift all these years, and where the hell were you when I should have been doing it?

Watching you blow it. When I had the time.

And when you didn't?

Oh, off fighting Romans and other oafs.

That's nice, Zenobia, cute.

I'm not a substitute for your head or your gut, I'm a gift, Gudrun, an extra. You should be glad you can still hear me. I'm telling you that girl was put in your way. You can waste us both if you wish, but I'm not sure how many more of us there'll be.

Us?

Yes. You want to talk about that or finish with Shithead? Oh yeah, I mean finish.

Maybe he's an advertising hotshot because his head is a Mardi Gras of images, maybe it's a carnival because he's an advertising hotshot. In any case the image Joe Feeney entertains these days of Artemisia is of a beautiful girl, younger than Artemisia, the moment just before she realizes her throat has been cut. He's probably seen such an outrage in a movie, but now, at all hours, he sees the knowledge of her death spread out from her pupils to the pales of her irises. He sees it in a mirror, standing behind her, because he is her assassin. In this

62

mirror the rest of his life is framed. He can't warn her, it's too late. Both of them are living in this gruesome instant of recognition. They're trapped in it. What he'd wanted from her, all he'd wanted, now seems a vulgar intrusion. He'd wanted love and with this wanting killed her.

The word kill has no arabesques and looks like a Kufic march of lancers and yet few words are as supple. The dead go about their business as usual, seen and unseen. Like Artemisia. Until now Joe thought it his business to dislodge Hereward Adamson as the head of Gossaert Nostrand. But now he recognizes his only purpose is to help Artemisia Cavelli adjust to her new station in . . . well, what can we call it? Her delusion? But he's not sure the man standing behind her in the mirror is up to the task because the man happens to have no reflection. She's the only person in the mirror. You have to be a bit more substantial than that to do what he has in mind. And, besides, he has already had far too much in mind where she's concerned.

But this is all in your head, Joe. Isn't that what his mother Terry always told him when she couldn't be bothered with his perceptions? It's all in your head. It took him many years to realize it couldn't have been anywhere else, but non sequiturs wouldn't have bothered Terry anyway. So here you are imagining standing behind Artemisia before a foggy bathroom mirror. Has she yet noticed you're not there, in the mirror? She's just zany enough not to say she notices. Yes, it's all in your head, Joseph. Terry would've said Joseph, because that was your name when you were an ass, which is what you grew up to be in spite of Terry's admonitions, what in fact makes you successful, such as success is. Once Terry assigns something to your head, that's it, pal, later for you.

He smiles. Sitting on a bench behind the New York Public Library watching the skaters in Bryant Park, he wonders how much of the world's literature has been about disabusing people of the insupportable notion they're alive. Could you really sell all that junk to living people? Would living people actually vote for the best liars they can find, or would a real life embolden them to imagine shouldering the great burden of wisdom? The circumstances that made him Joe and not Joseph discourage him now from indulging his true calling, philosophical inquiry. They didn't exactly say at Fordham that no one called Joe Feeney can be a philosopher, but it's the message he heard. A thug, a bartender, an IRA jerk-off, an advertising executive, those are Joe Feeney things. Not falling in love with Artemisia Cavelli, not marrying Nuala Gwilt and holding her footstool while she ascends to curatorial fame and power.

He's missed the boat. There are plenty of Irish names that would befit philosophers and poets. He doesn't have to be Italian or anything else, he simply needs a graver name. He has friends with just such names who went to Columbia and got the willies and dropped out when they encountered its provocative introduction to the humanities. He wouldn't have gotten the willies. He would have loved to X-ray the church, to question its fungal assumptions, but the Feeneys didn't have that kind of money, and Fordham's not too shabby.

I never feel like this name. Joseph Aloysius Feeney. Joe Feeney pumps hands and slaps backs on his way to the men's room. Joe Feeney shadowboxes with mailroom boys. Joe Feeney remembers the names of your kids. Joe Feeney goes to piano bars. Everybody loves Joe Feeney. Who the hell is Joe Feeney? I'll tell you one thing, it's not a featherweight question, because whoever the hell he is, he isn't showing up in the mirror anymore. And back when he did, I didn't know him. But you know what's funny about that? Everyone else acts like they know him.

He jumps up to help a kid who has crashed into the rail.

"You okay, pal? Attaboy, go get 'em."

Even the kid acts like he knows Joe Feeney.

I think ya better ask yourself, buddy, just who Nuala thought she was marrying. I mean, can you imagine a Sarah Lawrence Gwilt marrying a mick who hangs out at P.J. Clarke's? A mick who doesn't know Masaccio from Pinocchio? And, trust me, it's not because the guy is great in bed, which wouldn't have been one of Nuala's most critical criteria anyway. No, I think it's because Mr. No-Image here has the gift of awe. Don't knock it. Not many people have it. Joseph A. Feeney experiences awe. He's comfortable with it. Show him something new and different, something beautiful, and he'll like you for it, maybe even love you. You'll start to tremble and glow because he practically worships something you've shown him.

Unfortunately, Artemisia is among the wonders Nuala showed him. When Nuala first took Joe to the Metropolitan Museum he thought he'd died and gone to heaven. Nuala had to marry a man like that. He could listen to her and her artsy friends for ten lifetimes and never interrupt or become bored. It wasn't bankable, but it was a gift of great price, and Nuala knew it. Tell him how a painting can be transferred from its original canvas to another, how pinholes can be restored, how colors are made, and he'll listen like a little boy who's just gotten his first train set. And he'll remember. Every damned detail.

Now where'd all that go? It wasn't showing up in the mirror. It had gone off with him somewhere. Certainly not to Bryant Park.

The more he watches the skaters the more he sees himself as a concierge. He has to help Artemisia use the accommodations to which her premature arrival in an unfamiliar place has entitled her, and this role of concierge feels more like what he would have been had he not been handed his good-buddy name. This frozen body of shallow water in front of him represents the surface on which he's skated all his life, executing superficial turns and pro forma maneuvers, skating backwards to impress peers. It's a perfect metaphor for his roles as Mr. Nuala Gwilt and Master Joseph Feeney.

The sob in his chest feels as big as a medicine ball. He's gagging on it. He rubs it as he sits on his bench watching the skaters describe his life, a life of skittering over the shiny surface of things.

Sometimes when we throw our lives away we find a better one hidden in our belongings. Joe Feeney is about to acquire twenty of them. He decides he's hungry or ought to be. Hot dogs and falafels strike him as vomitous. But a piping pot of lemon curry shrimp at a Thai restaurant might take the chill out of his bones. He can throw his life away later. Anytime. He's good at it. Terry had a mantra about that. Joe will always find a way to shoot himself in the foot, trust me, she'd say. He'd examined Terry's mantra up and down and sideways. He didn't want his mother to be wrong. What kind of a world would it be if mothers were wrong about such important things?

His dad, Pat, who delivers beer to bars in jolly aluminum kegs, thinks Joe is a good guy, a decent sort of fellow, like Pat. What does he know? Pat doesn't know much, but he knows the IRA harbors murderers, and Joe gives the old man a lot of credit for not being delusional about that. He isn't a professional Irishman, isn't even usually taken for one. Joe is often mistaken for one, and when you're in advertising you don't like to disabuse people of their fondest follies, such as Irishness rubbing off on you. Something else about Pat Joe likes. His father actually thinks success is being kind, a bizarre notion—Joe worships him for it.

Terry on the other hand thinks rassling beer barrels a disgrace. She and Nuala wear the family pants and have a high regard for each other based on Terry's failure to notice that Nuala thinks her a termagant. Nobody knows it, but every night at the brewery when Pat washes up to go home, he mutters, Home it is, Patrick, to the Banshee. The Banshee is always capitalized in his mind, if only because he's sure there's no other banshee like her. It isn't in his nature to talk about her, or for that matter, to talk about anybody, but there are times when he'd like to tell someone a certain thing about Terry, and about himself, a certain thing he never understood. It wants telling, to someone. God knows, not a priest, not in confession. No, not to any paid listener.

When he and Terry were kids, she was a bossy girl with a face so radiant you could warm your hands on it on a winter's night. People in the neighborhood tranced around in a funk until they beheld that face. She was a rowdy girl without being a loudmouth. In his mind he always tried to supplant rowdy with randy, but Terry was never randy, she just went from rowdy to pot-banging. Still, she knows when to back off, because she's seen Pat when he's gotten into one of his terrors, as she puts it. The first time was in a Knights of Columbus hall at a dance. It wasn't Saint Patrick's Day, but the Irish, still dominating the parish, were in full throat, and two pugs from their block were pushing a spidery Puerto Rican kid around for making eyes at Maureen (Legs) O'Halloran, who was miffed at anybody who didn't make eyes at her. Pat, then nineteen, simply got up from their table, strode over to the fracas and banged the bullies' heads together, knocking them out cold on the floor. Young Father Isaac Coleman came over and said, Look whatcha did now, ya bloody boy.

"Ah, shut yer flaunty face," Pat said, "ya saw what the sons-a-bitches did with yer own eyes, Father, dincha?"

Joe's future parents were standing under a lamppost outside the K of C hall, Terry measuring him admiringly.

"Didja say f-l-a-u-n-t-y face, Patrick? D'ya know what it means? Ya mean faggot, Patrick," she said.

"Well, ya know I don't like confession, Theresa, but if ya wanna know, I read the dictionary in my spare time. Now don't say a word, will ya, just let it be."

Fat chance.

"The dictionary?"

"Yeah, well, wudja rather it be *Playboy* then?"

So Terry knew that although Pat grew up on the same side of the street, he was a man of secret parts. She was lucky to have gotten to know this much about him, considering their soiled past, because when they were children and she was bigger, for maybe three years, she'd run him down in vacant lots and abandoned warehouses, pin him to the ground with her knees, pull down her pungent britches and pee on him.

Now why in God's name, he wonders every day, would a man marry such a feral minx, unless of course he likes being pissed on. Pat doesn't. He wasn't a born underling. None of his peers at the brewery would pick a fight with The Patrick, as they were inclined to call him. If you picked a fight with Patrick Feeney you'd bloody well have to finish it, and that would mean making sure he didn't get up off the floor, which he sure as hell would if you'd gotten him down in the first place.

So that's what bothers him about the termagant. He needs to tell somebody about that preadolescent splattering. He thinks about it when he shaves. What about this face made the damn girl want to pee on it? It never occurs to him she might have anointed any number of faces, and probably some of them he socializes with every day. And that of course is what somebody would tell him if he could get up the nerve to talk about it. But then where would he be, surrounded by men indecently curious about his private life?

It never happened in their marriage, although he half expected it to. Not even when they were both shit-faced. In fact, Terry is a respectful lover, and grateful for his respect, which doesn't stop her from being what Nuala knows damn well she is. And that's one reason Pat liked Nuala from the start. Joe found a girl who didn't dick around with anybody. Or did she find Joseph? Maybe not the neighborhood's dish of tea. Certainly not the neighborhood's dish of tea. But a right person all the same, and Irish to boot. Not that being Irish is all that great to Pat. He thinks it accidental, although perhaps not quite as accidental as being Italian. He thinks pagan Irish would be better, but in his anticlericalism he's quite Sicilian. He thinks the Irish should remember Saint Patrick for the British imperialist he was. And he wonders why he didn't marry a Sicilian girl or a Polish girl or a Jewish girl. He'd certainly been attracted to quite a few of them. Lack of imagination, he tells his mirror. Now Joe had had some imagination, even if Nuala is disappointingly Irish. She isn't Irish Irish anyway, if you know what he means, which he doesn't exactly. But if you ask him he'll say something like, Well, her people didn't come from Limerick, now did they? In his mind coming from Limerick is worse than Orange. Come to think of it, he doesn't know, firsthand that is, what's so bad about Orange. That's the problem with being Irish, as he sees it, so much received bullshit. Did the Italians suffer the same, he wonders? Surely not. Their prejudice seems limited to the Irish, and that blessedly faded as the young Irish and Sicilians discovered each other.

68

He could not say why he had married Terry. Maybe he was engulfed in the sheer size of her liveliness, her peachy vividness, her pomegranate heartiness, the way her wild blue irises lassoed you into her pupils. She makes people blush, especially priests and nuns. She colors the life around her, connects the dots, makes empty rooms pulse, and yet Theresa Culhane doesn't claim anything not allotted to her. She leaves their proper space to others. Her only trespass, as far as Pat knows, is that obscenity committed against him in their childhood. Present at their marriage, at Joe's conception, a secret between them that neither of them understands. He can never see into it deeply enough to call it a Culhane tragedy, a darkness undoubtedly visited on Terry herself. It's why Pat looks pleadingly at Joe at table: You are the light of my life, so please shed some of it on this pain.

As for their daughter Marjorie, as bright of visage as Terry, only a year younger than Joe, Pat is content in his conviction that he's brought enough to the marriage to preclude her ever squatting on some miscreant like himself.

Joe misunderstands Pat's pleading look. He thinks Pat wants forgiveness for not having been a good enough father. He misunderstands because he thinks Pat is a superb father.

Appropriate to her new status as a blacklisted member of the undead, Artemisia is not answering phone calls or e-mails. The manager at Number Two Sutton Place South hasn't seen her in more than three weeks but reminds Joe that's not unusual. Her vintage baby blue Mercedes coupe is in her garage, but her black Lexus is gone.

Joe fancies Brooklyn Bridge a giant harp. Walking across it to Dumbo isn't going to pluck the dread out of his head, but it will allow the Fates to run their fingers through his hair and tell him how sorry they are his life has come to this, this task of having to tell Artemisia his love for her has destroyed her dreams. It doesn't occur to him that he doesn't know what Artemisia dreams.

He takes a cab from his office at Madison and 56th to the foot of the bridge and starts walking. Artemisia might be in her two-story loft on Water Street in the embrace of the two bridges. She'll be walking around barefoot in splattered blue coveralls and a white T-shirt, her hair piled on top of her head to keep it out of her paints. She'll be making the rounds of a dozen palettes where she mixes paints. Four or five huge canvases will be suspended from the ceiling. No, that's not quite right. They're canvas contraptions. Each has several planes. To make them she has to be as good a carpenter and electrician as she is a painter. They're planes within planes, illuminated from all four sides to create shadows. The slight movement of these devices suspended on fish-line orchestrates their shadows. This restless invention had moved Nuala to call her a Twenty-First-Century Da Vinci. Joe had teased Nuala about it.

"Don't you think that's a bit over the top?"

"No, I don't. Have you seen her drawings? She's one of the few contemporaries who can draw. She draws every damned detail. Her drawings are better than the work she shows."

"So why don't you exhibit her drawings?"

"She won't let me. She won't show them. They're her private language. The girl has secrets, Joe, lots of secrets."

And if you want to attract Nuala Gwilt you need every secret you can lay hands on, and it needs to be clear you aren't going to give them up, even for fame. Some people, usually women, are fragrant with secrets, but Artemisia bore them the way some people have green thumbs. They have them and you're glad.

When most men fantasize about women, they're making love or something that passes for it, or they're humiliating someone, but Joe's enduring fantasy concerning Artemisia is the two of them walking around: he's showing her his favorite things and she's sketching them.

He can't imagine anything more fulfilling and he can't share this longing with a single soul, because, things being what they are, it's taboo. So now he'll tell Artemisia, but only because he has to tell her he's ruined her. Nuala has ruined her, but Joe had been given, had accepted responsibility for the balance of their—what was it? not a ménage, not a friendship, nothing as indifferent as a relationship—and so he has ruined everything.

70

As he approaches her building he remembers her installations being moved out of it by men in white coats. Newspapers and magazines devoted space to the feat.

Joe remembers fondly a *New York Times* photographer who confided to him at one of Artemisia's openings:

"You know, I have the damnedest feeling that if I don't sneak up on that girl she won't be there when I go to shoot. I mean she's a little . . ."

"Ghostly?"

"Yeah, ghostly. You know her?"

"My wife and I have vacationed with her on the Vineyard."

The photographer had looked at Joe as if to say, Well, that's not exactly what I asked, but I'll take it as a yes. He shouldn't have. Taken it as a yes. Neither Joe nor Nuala know Artemisia, they just want to bask in her boreal light. In fact, Joe isn't at all sure anyone knows Artemisia or can know her. He loves her, but he doesn't really want to make love to her. He doesn't want anyone to. She isn't that sort of being at all. She has no carnal side, not even naked. Of course it's possible other men and women see her and feel differently, but Nuala isn't one of them. She adores Artemisia. Artemisia is to her what Haley Pennock was to Artemisia. They don't want to wear Artemisia, to be seen with her, it isn't like that. It wasn't like that. She was a secret privilege they wanted to have. Nuala felt entitled to this privilege. Joe felt included.

The cheetah is the fastest animal, sometimes achieving bursts of more than sixty miles an hour. She stirs admiration in us, but not primeval dread. She lives in Africa and Asia. We associate her with heat. She doesn't inspire malaise. Her beauty delights but doesn't transfix us. The wolf, bounding on the crusted snows of our subconscious, nearer magnetic north, her we associate with dread. Our relationship with her is ancient and haunted.

Gudrun Kierstadt, overwhelmed by a reverie of wolves, doesn't recognize that it's inspired by a specific wolf, one she has just seen.

A skater whooshes past her on her way to the Naumberg Bandshell in Central Park. Out of the corner of her left eye she sees a white flash. When she turns she sees a wolf hurtling benches and snow fences, keeping up with the skater.

No sooner she sees this wolf than she thinks of wolves in dream mist. The wolf, she knows, prowls what we abandon and makes dogs whine. We can hardly imagine fear without the wolf. He consorts with vampires. He worried us when we lived at campfires. We remember it.

And here she is, keeping pace with a tall red-haired girl in ragged denim cutoffs and blue crash helmet, loping along with that loose, elegant gait that distinguishes her.

By the time Gudrun recognizes that her consideration of cheetahs and wolves is prompted by a real wolf, girl and wolf are gone. She hurries along the path, hoping forlornly to find them again. Just before she comes to the bandshell she sees the wolf sitting at the foot of an elm, waiting for her, not for the girl, but for Gudrun. She slows down and approaches. The wolf's sapphire eyes survey her. When she is only three or four feet away she notices passersby with their dogs. They walk by brusquely, but the dogs glance sidelong, wince, cringe and whine.

The dogs see you, don't they? But the people don't. Are you curious why I see you? That's what I do, but it brings me only misery. I see what others can't see. Sometimes I hear people think. I live in hell. But you're not from hell, are you? I know you're not. Where's your friend? Take me to your friend. Please.

They walk sedately, side by side, to the bandshell, where Artemisia is skating. She whisks past them once. When she comes around again she spins in the air and comes down facing them.

They begin to talk—Gudrun will never remember how they begin—and then they're interrupted by two mounted policemen clattering across the mall after a purse-snatcher. They try to talk but are separated by a crowd being herded out of the bandshell area by cops on foot. When Gudrun is able to turn around, the girl and the wolf are gone.

Shithead has husbanded the Kierstadt fortune with prescient genius. But it remains Kierstadt money, as family lawyers engineered from the start. He's entitled to all he made with it, as far as Gudrun is concerned. He's shuffled funds from equities to mutuals, mutuals to hedges, hedges to bonds, bonds to realty trusts, copper to emeralds, emeralds to gas, ceaselessly vigilant, predatory as a bald eagle.

Even Gudrun has made them richer, buying art cleverly, donating it for power and for tax shelters, playing the market, winning big at auction, deaccessioning overstuffed museums and reselling smartly as a private dealer. Perhaps her ESP gives her the edge, but these games of greed demean it.

Gudrun heard the veil of illusion rip when she was a girl and ignored it in the tumult of hormones. That, at least, is the favored view of self-involved mothers. She knows she'd become face-blind and that in recompense the faces people wear behind their official fronts appear to her. Now she has to devise her own mnemonics to recognize others. Pretending not to see what clearly she does see takes its toll. Instead of aging and tiring she becomes unknowable and unmemorable. Money is the marker by which people remain conscious of her, but she recedes behind it.

She has always thought that being unable to conceive was the price she had to pay for penetrating the veil. It doesn't make medical sense, but not much does. When she realizes it's a gift, she understands Shithead must be left to his devices. But what are hers? Somewhere between the zoo and the bandshell is the answer. She knows that even more surely than she knows the next painting to buy.

She arrives at her chosen bench at five-thirty-five in the morning. If she'd bothered to look in her mirror she'd have noticed that her face, an arrangement of rectangles, sexual in the graven severity of the whole, has softened, like moist clay awaiting human thumbs. She gobbles down a big warm pretzel, drinks a little water from a fountain, and settles in for her wait. She is studying *The Bridge* by Hart Crane, as she has studied such projects for years. It assumes a certain cogency in her mind because there's an elderly East Side artist whose big abstract acrylics are influenced by the city's bridges, especially the Manhattan and Brooklyn, and Gudrun plans to buy the lot of them.

Just before eight o'clock Thunder materializes on Gudrun's bench to the left. Gudrun slips her paperback into her coat pocket and together they stare ahead, motionless. In a few minutes Artemisia sails by on in-line skates, a small sketchpad tucked behind her waistband. Three feet past them she jumps into the air, as she had on the band shell's mall, and lands facing them.

"You do see my wolf!"

"Is she yours?"

"Well, now that you ask, perhaps I'm her human."

"For lack of a better word?"

They laugh. Yes, this is the moment Gudrun has been looking for. This is why she came here.

"My name is Gudrun Kierstadt. Do I look like one?"

"A Gudrun Kierstadt?"

"Mmm."

"You look like a person who makes me wonder what else you can see. I'm Artemisia Cavelli. I'm an artist."

"Of course you would be."

They laugh again.

"You remind me of Haley Pennock, my grandmother."

"Is that good, Artemisia?"

"It's blessed."

"The Haddon Pennocks? Haddon & Lillibridge?"

"Yes, exactly."

"Let's have some hot dogs."

"Do you skate, Gudrun?"

"I'd like to."

"Good, we'll rent some skates and we'll see where Thunder leads us."

"Far from where I've been, I hope."

"You hear that, Thunder? May I ask you to arrange it?"

"Does she do as you ask?"

"I don't know. I doubt it. I've never asked her for anything. We'll see."

74

Artemisia is their compass. Without her they have to navigate point to point and can hardly find the market. They sit propped against a rough-parged brick wall in their studio in the Eagle Warehouse, listening to the trains on the Manhattan Bridge, the rumble and bluster of traffic on Dumbo's cobblestone streets. They imagine they can smell the nutmeg and cardboard that had been housed in the neighborhood, the tar of the ships creaking on their dock lines, the gum arabic of the *Brooklyn Eagle,* whose presses once shook their muscular brick building. But all they can really hear are their hearts' panicky tattoo.

What freezes them is the chance that a lightning bolt has severed the part of Artemisia's brain that loves and shelters them from another part that may harbor unease with their improbable relationship. Everything feels more foreign than before. Their clothes hurt. The sun barges in on their brains and turns far reaches into deserts. The city clangs in their ears. Brooklyn Bridge to the south and Manhattan Bridge to the north threaten to fall on them. Everything's too loud, too big, too bright. The phones tremble with dread. They're being deported from their jerrybuilt lives. They sit trying to remember Alberta's wheat fields at dusk, the lights of the combines blinking, the northern lights like an electrocardiograph on the horizon. They try to remember the farmhouse outside Red Deer that Edward Hopper might have painted on summer evenings. They try to see themselves ghosting between each other's bedrooms in the twilight. But all their memories run from them like mercury.

Artemisia made everything right, made it work. Where there was nowhere to go she opened a path. Where there was only nakedness and humiliation, she clothed and warmed them. But it always worried them they had so little to give her, that she seemed to need so little. They put it down to her otherness, to fate having brought them together. But it had always been a flimsy rationale, and now it has fallen into a crack in the sky.

Artemisia might be no more than three blocks west on Water Street in her airy loft, or across the river on Sutton Place, but even if they find her, does she want to be found? They imagine her not recognizing them or telling them things have changed.

Delia rises and walks over to her worktable. She picks up two fat black markers.

"Peter, in our best script we're going to write the names of all the people who've ever meant anything to us. All of them. Fetch the ladder. We'll start at the ceiling. Don't forget anyone. Then we'll go back and color them, whatever color comes to mind. This is very important, Peter, I know it, I'm sure."

"And then what?"

"We'll sit down right here and we'll decide if we need any of them."

"If they need us?"

"Maybe that too, I don't know. We'll see, Peter. This isn't a plan, it's a leap. If we don't need any of them, we'll just go. We can do that, can't we?"

"If Artemisia were doing this, Delia, she'd also write down things, like her paintings. And even if she didn't color us in such a way that told her she needed us, we'd still be her project, something for her to do."

"We don't have projects, Peter. We're not even our own project, the way we are Artemisia's. I don't have to finish any of the restorations over there. You don't have to give your next lecture. We don't even have to, to . . . well, we don't even have to love one another. We do, yes, but is it urgent, does it matter?"

"It's always been urgent enough to exclude everybody else, Delia. Yes, there have been others, but did we ever want to go back to them, to live with them, even for a little while?"

She hands him a marker.

"Write, Peter. Climb up to the top and write. It doesn't matter one bit what Artemisia would do. We already know she isn't anything like us."

"But more like us than anyone else."

"Well, that sounds good, dear heart, but I'm not sure it's right, because she isn't like anybody else, and we both knew that the moment we saw her. So write."

"My column first, then yours? So the same names will appear twice?"

"Yes, I think that's the best way."

Sunlight rams huge girders into the unlit studio. Delia picks her way between them, undressing, scattering her clothes across the floor. The scent of rotten orange and the mown-hay odor of linseed rise to the ceiling. He looks down to see Delia standing naked with buttery coils of oil paint on her left thigh: alizarin crimson, cadmium yellow, cadmium selenide, Prussian blue. This barbarous vision has visited him before, but not in this life. Tears fill his mouth, but the only taste he wants is his sister's, her wild and forever unattainable tastes. She stands looking at him, painting in the air with a delicate sable brush. He starts to come down, but she wags a forefinger at him.

"You are always unattainable, Delia," he blurts.

She turns and walks away into the sun.

The pine tar of turpentine incites a space with expectancy, varnish seals a moment with amber reassurances—his list of names grows. So far he needs none of them.

It doesn't occur to either of them that their lists must end with each other's names.

Delia taps the bottom of the ladder.

"You can't, we can't write Artemisia's name down, Peter. That's the point. Her people have taken her. That's what we have to suppose. They've taken her back and left a facsimile. We have nothing to do with the facsimile."

He nods. It's a good thing he doesn't have to list the things he's initiated in his life, because he can't think of one such thing. Delia is the initiator. But Peter, able athlete, sociable, almost everyone's idea of a fine fellow, is her front man. She's certainly many people's fancy of desirable, but in truth, or maybe as a mere matter of pheromones, not many people do desire her, and fewer still imagine making love to her, which is not the same as wanting her. We often want people we wouldn't know what to do with. Not counting Artemisia, who could never be counted in any group.

Artemisia and Delia often smell alike, hanging around the same chemicals as they do, but their body humors make a special alchemy that haunts their relationships with others. For Peter it's the bouquet of safety. For Nuala it's the suspicion Artemisia's genealogy is a lie, that her origins are a disturbance of natural order. For Joe it's the memory of something out of mind's reach, centuries past. Everyone who desires Artemisia believes but would never say that, together, they make a glorious androgyne.

With one-inch flat brushes they've colored almost half the names on their wall when they feel a chill in the room. Manhattan looks like a forest fire as the sun falls behind it. But the room is cold. Now Peter undresses. They paint each other as they decide how to color the people who've come and gone in their lives. Their glances begin to prize open dark corners, looking for the cold presence that has invaded them.

"I think we've conjured something, Delia. We've stumbled on some kind of conjuration. We're not alone."

"No, you're not."

Artemisia closes the distance from the door to them with her usual kick-ball stride. She picks up a marker from the floor and scrawls her name, slanting upward, to the left of their two columns of names.

"What color am I?"

They fling themselves on her.

She had let herself in silently after Thunder, who merely passed through the wall. She had stood awhile leaning against the door frame, watching, listening, figuring out what they were doing, enjoying them.

Now she too starts to undress, dropping the clothes they ruined with their painted bodies.

"Let's get on with it, then. Let's see what happens when we've written them all down. I'm up for this. But listen, my darlings, I'm yours, you're mine. And we have a new friend. I saw you looking for her. Her name is Thunder. She's my wolf. Um, actually I'm her person. She'll be your friend, don't worry, don't ever worry."

"Um, um, ah, Artemisia . . ."

"Yes, Peter, I was. I was listening. For a long time. But I don't think you ever have any thoughts that would offend me. I was resting. I needed to watch people I love."

When Joe spots her she is walking backwards beckoning to someone he can't see. There's no one else on the sidewalk, but he still can't see the object of Artemisia's gesturing. She's wearing blue hospital scrubs splotched with paint and brown hiking boots. Rags hang out of her back pockets. She spreads her arms wide as if to catch something thrown. Then she spins around and sees Joe.

She strides up to him and presses her forehead to his.

"I can't touch you. I'm full of paint. I've been to see Delia and Peter and we're working on a huge project. But it's secret. You're part of it. We've written your name on a wall, but I forget how we colored you. It's very esoteric. I don't understand it at all, but I will. I'll take you to see it one day. You look like you just saw a ghost. Do I look like a ghost, Joe? I'd understand. I have a lot to tell you. How is dear Nuala?"

"Uh, ah, Artemisia, I, I have something awful to tell you."

"Before I wash up? Do we need to be outdoors?"

"Yes, that would be good."

"Do you think we unerringly find what's bad for us and spend the rest of our lives groaning about our bad luck?"

Artemisia was up, as usual, with dawn, and sits cross-legged watching the sun set the windows of Manhattan on fire. Joe got up later and quietly set about making them breakfast. Now he comes up behind her with coffee.

"I don't think that's what we're doing, Joe. I think most of us are struck by lightning of some sort and spend the rest of our lives pretending it didn't happen. We catch the breaks, but they scare us off. You know, the way I scare you."

She looks up at him, smiling. They'd spent the night in each other's arms and now can't say anything happened and can't say anything hasn't.

"I like being scared. I always have. It feels like watching the dial of the compass coming around to true north. So I don't know why I put those damned pictures in the safe. Behind Gorky, no less. Gorky, who wasn't meant to hide anything."

"So I could scare you in private?"

He kisses the top of her head. "No, I think it was to make trouble. I think I needed trouble. I sure as hell made it, didn't I? How can you stand being here with me?"

"I don't know if you made it—you know, the trouble—or Pan made it. I think it was Pan who threw that lightning bolt at me. I'm not even sure it's trouble we're looking at. Have you been feeling the draft?"

"Uh, now that you mention it, I turned over a few times during the night and I saw—I dunno, this is crazy—I thought I saw a white arc in different corners of the loft and then I started shivering."

"It's not crazy, it's Thunder. Life is about glimpses into what's too right or too wrong and what we don't do about them. It's what I try to paint. Thunder's job seems to be to show me what's happening as opposed to everybody else's official story. Words are no good for that. I have to follow her."

"She brought you down off the mountain?

"No. I was too badly hurt. A diminutive ranger was up there building gabions. She whipped together a travois, and as we descended I noticed Thunder tracking us in the woods. I told the ranger I'd heard there were no wolves left in the Catskills. She looked over at Thunder's blue eyes and nodded. The common wisdom of rangers often flies in the face of public policy."

"I was thinking about strangling Nuala with her bra, Artemisia."

"I'll bet you were thinking someone other than you would be thinking about it. Joe, the trouble is she's disappointed in herself. Her favorite perfumes are going to stink. A quaver in her voice will betray her schemes. She'll start watching the phone. The phone will fill up the whole room. There won't be any room for her. Her Blackberry will fill with inconsequence. She's taken a wrong turn. Nobody casts us in these parts, Joe. We don't have to play them. It's Nuala's script. We have other work to do, don't we? Isn't that what you proposed?"

"And then we have to go home?"

"Or not. You can get in a lot of trouble trying to go home to a home you never had. Cardboard boxes and doorways and crannies under trestles are full of people who didn't go home. And if they had they might have killed somebody."

"The lightning woke up the extra cells in your brain, Artemisia."

"I think it switched on my willingness to act on what I know."

"I'm never sure if the way I see something is the way it really is. Maybe it is, if only for the moment. We can't live pretending we know how things are. I don't trust people who know the score. I think most of the time we're acting on bad intelligence."

"I do think life is impossible, Joe. And that makes us miracles, don't you think? I always feel I'm snatching something out of the void when I paint. It doesn't belong to me. I'm a thief. But not my own thief. If I exhibit it, I'm fencing it. You know, I don't feel as if I was hit by lightning, I feel as if I was snatched from a world I wasn't supposed to be in, and now I'm sort of living in between, in a crack between worlds. Let me go get my backpack and we'll take that walk, the one you said you wanted from me, the one we were meant to take."

Then the cracked artist and the uncertain pornographer set out into the city that had been vengefully ruined for them.

When you have money it's easy to imagine you could have managed without it, or less of it. Not that money makes everything easier. It doesn't. It makes trust and friendship harder. It makes it harder for people to see you, and sometimes they can't see you at all for the money, and you can't see them either. It's as if you're always peering around piles of loot.

Artemisia had never thought about Haley's wealth, so when Haley died and left it to her she was angry. It was such a mean substitute for Haley, such an empty token, a token of emptiness. It deafened her to Haley's biggest gift to her, her repeated admonition that nothing needs to happen, nothing depends on anything happening.

So Artemisia went out blessedly into the world without a sense that something, anything, must happen. So imbued

81

with this freedom was she that each thing that did happen, each person happening along, enjoyed her attention and good will. She didn't see anything or anyone as the hinge on which everything hung.

For this reason she's the person Gudrun needs to meet, the exact person. More accurately, she's the person to whom Thunder needs to bring Gudrun. No telling why, of course. And that leads to Haley's next gift. Haley had no patience with whys. It didn't matter why. She didn't like whys and she didn't like rhetorical questions. Because she never quibbled with events, and because she was Artemisia's model, Artemisia never quibbled with what the day brought her. Of course she made judgments and spoke her mind, although infrequently, but mostly she watched, like Thunder.

One must never bully one's own mind, Artemisia, Haley had said. There's no use staging debates in your head when you could be listening to sonatas. We're not noisy persons, you and I. Just because your mouth is shut doesn't mean you're not a noisy person. You can see that in people's eyes, dear. Have you ever noticed some people have eyes that are hard to see, no matter how hard you try . . . avoid them. And exhibitionists, well, their eyes are just sea glass.

Gudrun's amber eyes are haunted by afterimages. Her eyes frisk people's auras. Money buys Gudrun time to know her own mind. She doesn't hide behind wealth.

"I understand the craziness of bag ladies, Artemisia. They stay focused on whatever they're snatching up or hoarding because impressions assault them with great velocity and volume. The aggravating little thing they're obsessed with is their defense for not having filters. They can't filter all the impressions that come at them. Neither can I, but I pass for formidable on account of being rich. People have their expectations, and sometimes there's no sense in disabusing them. I have this wonderful doorman who's unusual among doormen because he's not obsequious. I feel responsible for the man, because I know he needs to kiss ass to make money. You could say my life is a huge failure if my chief responsibility seems to be a dignified doorman."

82

"I wouldn't say it, Gudrun. No, on the contrary."

Artemisia's entire body responds to this remark about the doorman. She feels hot, then cold. She looks around and sees Thunder sitting behind Gudrun, lowering her beautiful head as if receiving a benediction. Yes, that's what it is, Gudrun's story. She's like Artemisia. She cares about people whose integrity puts them in danger, people whose station in life can't protect their innocence.

"I'm going to be a bag lady out here, Artemisia. I've seen it coming for a long time. I see, I feel what's up ahead, but I've never known what to do about it. I meet people whose minds I hear. I read them as clearly as tabloid headlines. The ink is in the air. Their faces fall off and there they are, standing right in front of me, their real faces cycling, tiger to hyena, hyena to ferret, ferret to grizzly, grizzly to serpent, serpent to half-human, would-be human faces, and faces that won't hold their shapes at all. Some people think like Mozart or Titian, and you'd be amazed where you find such people. In doorways on cold nights. If I didn't hear them I'd have died a long time ago."

Artemisia sits and unlaces her well-worn skates. Then, slinging them over her shoulder, she takes Gudrun's hand.

"Come, let's walk a bit. I have something for you to do. Someone needs your help. She's concerned with the way the elements pass, water over stone, light through glass, wind through trees and grass. She wants to be one with these passages. She feels instinctively we get into trouble when we stand in the way of passages. She thinks our thoughts and actions are viral, airborne. I have a friend who thinks he killed me with his desire, Gudrun. Killed me by liking me too much. He thinks I'm a dead girl walking. I think our energies aren't so easily sorted out. His wife has found him out, bumbled into his head and found me naked there, and now she's in a self-righteous snit. But she's wanted me all along. She wants him as a witness, she wants him to feel what she has trouble feeling, to grieve, to fear, to lust, but not to have, because having would be an overstatement, a misstep in the cutting of a jewel."

"And neither one of them has a clue who you are! I'm right about that, aren't I, Artemisia?"

"She thinks unless I'm safely in her possession I'm a danger to them. I suppose she's right, only because she is who she is. She knows enough to delight in the precarious balance of things, but she thinks she has to possess the balance, like one of those brass clocks in a glass. She doesn't know she can't. He half-sees Thunder, Gudrun. And given the opportunity, she couldn't see Thunder. It could be we all have a being by our side like Thunder, and it could be almost everyone in our lives is blind to it. I don't know. How many people know what you hear? How many would believe it? The few assumptions I had are splintered. Nothing's the same. The lightning changed everything. But I know you see Thunder, and I know she sits near you, and that's not her habit. The scent of your spirit is good. I don't know where she was before lightning struck. Or what she was. But I know everything has the imminent odor of ozone, and nothing I do niggles anymore. You know that smell? I call it something-must-happen-ness. It's exciting, but you can't take it as a constant state.

"You'd die young. Something else I see about you, Gudrun, your mouth. It's a straight line. You probably think it's too thin, too austere. But if you're going to listen to people think, you have to have a mouth like that, one that doesn't give any clues."

She'd taken Gudrun with her right hand, but now Gudrun switches around behind her, takes her left hand and squeezes it hard. She's taller than Artemisia and looks down at the perfectly straight part in Artemisia's fiery hair with a profound fondness. She studies the thin scar racing down Artemisia's forehead to her brow. Sometimes love is too antique a word for what you feel for someone, a lame word we've had to leave behind. She leaves the word behind and kisses the part in Artemisia's hair.

Her apartment on Fifth Avenue, her art dealings belong to a distant cousin's life. She doesn't even want to consign them, because she doesn't want them back, no matter what price they might bring. She and Artemisia are mad, both of them, exactly as they should be in the presence of Thunder. They don't need to know a thing about each other, a state familiar to Artemisia but a revelation to Gudrun.

"You're the sort of person people want to ascribe secrets to, Artemisia. But I think you have none. I think you have only privacies. I think some people are eaten up by these secrets you don't have, Artemisia. This must trouble you. You must often feel you're being mugged, rifled."

"We're both like Greek statues time has stripped bare. People want to color us so they can see who we are. They want to color us so they can define us, to cubbyhole us."

"Oh God, what a forlorn hope!"

They thrust their clasped hands forward and skip like girls. Thunder, running ahead, turns and stretches herself back from her forepaws, arching her back. They stop to watch her. She comes up to Artemisia and holds a surprisingly big paw up. Artemisia presses it with a palm.

"Did you know that the Catskills are one of the most hydrographically complex systems in the world? That's where I met Thunder. She was leaping over freshets and kills when the lady ranger hauled me down the mountain in a travois."

Thunder leads them to Seventy-second Street and Fifth Avenue, where they buy dirty-water dogs and cream sodas from a pushcart. They sit on the park side watching the stroller moms panzer their kids through beleaguered humanity. Gudrun waits for Artemisia to say what she'd come to hear, having no idea what it is. Artemisia waits for the impulse to say it. She stares down Seventy-second Street, looking for the idea. A Londonesque green tour bus bears down westward on the park.

"I have a friend who lives in a crystal cave. Like Merlin. Well, actually it's a green fluorite cave. Up in Lewis County near the Saint Lawrence. Her name is Gladys Moon. She was my grandmother Haley's friend. We started going up there when I was nine. Gladys believes fluorite amplifies her prayers. She believes it draws the mind away from obsessions that make us sick. I got the best ideas for some of my work sitting alone in her cave while Gladys was out working on her grounds. My thoughts just . . . well, they crystallized."

"And she lives in this cave?"

"Oh, it has all the conveniences. She installed light and air tunnels, and it's heated geothermally from copper coils in wells. But the cave is only part of the place's spell, Gudrun. We should visit Gladys. I have an idea you'll like her. You might even like to stay and work with her. And she hasn't met Thunder."

"Will she see her?"

"I have no doubt. Her hundred and twenty acres is what Frederick Law Olmsted and Calvert Vaux would have done with Central Park if they'd consulted a Merlin. She sinks long aluminum coffers filled with crystals into streambeds and seals them with Lucite covers. The refracted lights under the rushing water make you gasp. Most of the crystals are clear, but some are amethyst and green and amber. In deserted woodpecker holes she embeds amber and green glass. She lines streambeds with Ulster County bluestone and etches personal hieroglyphs and poems in them. In a deep pine wood she built a glass hangar and filled it with paper sculpture and mobiles. Whatever hour you approach, it looks like a congress of wraiths."

"How did Haley meet her? Were they childhood friends?"

"My grandmother thought it bad policy to speak of origins, of beginnings. She thought it sets the terms for our dealings with each other, whereas the terms change every second. I sort of think of her idea as putting a Josef Albers in a baroque gilt frame. You wouldn't do it, but you wouldn't want to bother explaining why you wouldn't do it, either."

Gudrun laughed till she hiccupped. She thought of the little Albers in her apartment foyer.

"Oh, you wouldn't do it, Artemisia, unless you thought you could torture Albers in hell. But I like him, so I wouldn't want to. About Haley and Gladys, you don't know or you're not telling?"

"I never answer questions I don't like, Gudrun, and I have a feeling you do and it's not good for you. Who do you have to answer to? I think you need some green fluorite."

Gudrun is stricken. By Artemisia's answer, the dumb persistence that elicited it. Is this the way she is? Is it Gudrun she really needs to leave behind, not Shithead? Is he just an artifact? And how to heal this wound she's inflicted upon her friendship with this treasurable girl?

"I'm so terribly sorry, Artemisia. It was so rude of me. Apparently this is the way I am . . . regrettable."

"I think you don't like being put on, Gudrun. Neither do I. I was telling you the truth."

"I know. The difference between us is you know what it is and I don't."

"Oh, I think it's pretty ordinary to know it, but acting on it is another thing. Gladys once told me my plans get in the way of what wants to happen. What wants to happen is in the air. We feel it on our skins, but we do almost anything to ignore it, because we're sure it's not what we want to happen."

"I wanted you to happen, Artemisia. And now you're talking about Gladys Moon, so that's also what I sensed in the air, right?"

"Whatever weans the mind from its fearfulness, if only for a moment, Gladys embraces. I was visiting her once, it was on a college break, and I was bursting with plans, the way you either do at college, or you don't and get suicidal. You're the plan, Artemisia, she said, you. Just be still and listen. That's what I was doing when the lightning struck."

"How did you come by your name, Artemisia? My name, Gudrun, belongs to a Valkyrie."

A powerful reason stands in the way of answering Gudrun, but Artemisia doesn't know the reason, she just feels its imperative. She stretches her long legs out and grips the bench behind her.

Franco Cavelli, twenty-nine years old when he died, had been an artist. He'd fathered Artemisia out of wedlock with Barbara, her mother. He was already married to a fellow artist, Sosa. He and Barbara had met in the Uffizi Gallery in Florence. He was lecturing about its creator, Giorgio Vasari, architect and biographer of artists. From the moment Barbara knew she was pregnant he was determined to name the baby after Artemisia

Gentileschi, the Renaissance artist. He was sure the baby would be a girl. Barbara, just another rich tourist and already engaged to someone back in New York, had no idea who Gentileschi was, but she had heard of Vasari's *Lives of the Artists.*

She thought she'd embarked on a great lark and probably wouldn't have been deterred to know that Gentileschi's father taught her to paint but practically sold her to a fellow artist who raped her. It had all happened long ago and was of no concern to a debutante.

Three days after Artemisia was born Franco was poisoned. The police in Milan, where he and Sosa lived, called it food poisoning. Barbara, understandably, pointed the finger at Sosa, but the police figured Barbara got what she deserved, although they thought fate might have been more merciful to the handsome Lombard artist.

In any case, Artemisia entered the world with Gentileschi's triumphant name and the beauty of two foolish parents. Barbara hadn't a clue what family name the girl ought to bear. In fact, she was inclined to deposit her in some Milanese institution. But, being easily panicked, she conferred with Haley by phone, and Haley insisted immediately on two courses of action: bring the child home and give her her father's name, to hell with the wife. Home? Barbara had asked. Where was the child's home? Oh, for the love of God, Barbara, Haley had said, take some responsibility for once in your life. Barbara said, Mother, you don't understand, he had an Italian name.

Haley had loved to tell this story. So did Artemisia. Bring me my granddaughter, Haley had said.

It was too much to ask. Barbara, at that point, hardly knew how to get up in the morning, so she didn't bother. Haley Pennock flew to Milan and retrieved them both.

Artemisia didn't dislike the poisoner story. After all, Haley had liked it well enough to tell it, and she wasn't a storyteller. It was plausible and romantic, a bit too romantic for Artemisia's taste. She was picky about who heard it. Delia and Peter knew it. Nuala and Joe didn't. You never know who or what you're going to poison with information. Each relationship carries in it some word or look that can kill it. Artemisia is very good at detecting just which word and look. But she couldn't tell you how she'd come by such grim vigilance. Perhaps it was her way of explaining why she hadn't pleased Barbara enough to inspire the twit to bring her up.

Nonetheless she considered it her good fortune Barbara had dumped her on Haley, or rather Haley had never relinquished her after fetching her in Milan. Haley had only technically been her grandmother. In every other way Haley had been her mother. She doubted very much Barbara had given her a thought when she flew off a ski course at Banff and destroyed herself. After all, she'd hardly given anyone else a thought in her twenty-four years.

Haddon Pennock had died similarly, crashing his own plane while on a business trip over the Andes. Haley had spoiled Barbara, paying little attention until she realized too late the girl had inherited her parents' good looks but not their brains. She determined from the second week of Artemisia's life she would not spoil her granddaughter, but the two of them shared from the very first moment such a common sense of humor that the issue never arose.

"Let's drive up to see Gladys, okay?"
Gudrun smiles. Artemisia isn't telling. Gudrun isn't pushing.

"Miss Cavelli?"
"Yes."
"This is Letitia Alonzo in the director's office at The Chance? We have some of your small paintings in the office which we'd like you to come get?"
"All right. I think I know which ones they are. I'll make arrangements and get back to you, Miss Alonzo. Where is Nuala's assistant?"
"Which one would that be?"
"Oh, all right. I think I'll just come over this afternoon and get this over with. Where shall I come?"
"You can come directly to the director's office."
"Right. Thanks."

Officious chickies are a fact of life in New York City. A whole subspecies of assholes finds it convenient, chic even, to hide behind them. These chickies can tell an off-the-rack suit from a six-thousand-dollar Brioni, but they uniformly fail to fathom that old money doesn't advertise.

Artemisia had never encountered a Letitia Alonzo at the museum or, for that matter, a chickie. She assumed Nuala had gone out of her way to find one to sic on her. No special arrangements were needed. The small oils from her student days would fit nicely in a cab. Nuala wished to put her through this sad ordeal.

She made two decisions to cheer herself up. First, she'd wear her usual paint-spattered blue coveralls, white T-shirt and ankle boots. Second, she'd take the subway to Union Square, have herself a nice leisurely lunch and then stroll up to the museum.

This strategy worked well until she passed the mini-park the city had required of some developer next to the museum. Silky water sheeted a black granite wall, the authorized swank for such floral insertions. The park was peopled by a bag lady, the usual coffee-clutchers, smokers, and other escapees.

Artemisia had already returned her gaze to the street when she realized she'd seen Nuala in the park. She looked again and saw Nuala, ankles crossed, sitting on a slab of granite. She was staring fixedly at the west wall of the museum.

At the same moment Artemisia realized that Thunder had not come with her. Something about Letitia Alonzo's phone call had disconnected her from Thunder. She walked by the museum and bought a hot chocolate in the atrium of a nearby office building.

Not like Nuala to sit in a park. Maybe she was just avoiding a confrontation with Artemisia, but what confrontation would that be? Artemisia would greet her cordially, if not warmly, and she knew that.

She went back to the park. Nuala hadn't moved. She walked up to her and stood silently about two feet away. When Nuala finally turned to look up her face was blasted. It reminded Artemisia of the ecstasy of a Seville flamenco dancer, but it was a paroxysm of grief. Slowly her pupils drowned. She tried to say Artemisia's name, but her lips stuck open. Artemisia sat next to her.

"You're dead, you know."

Almost any answer would have killed. Nuala saw (imagined?) sheet lightning in Artemisia's eyes and thought, I never knew her. I never knew anything. My assumptions feel like pee in my shoes.

Nuala studied her erstwhile friend's mouth, the upper lip a Mary Rose longbow, the lower lip its string.

"If you'd have let me have the drawing of Haley everything would have been all right," she said.

"Mmm."

Artemisia coaxed Nuala's legs onto the granite bench with the back of her left hand. Then she pulled Nuala by the shoulders down into her lap. She wiped away Nuala's tears with her fingers and smiled. Then she searched Nuala's brows and eye sockets for places where her pain was stored. She pressed them. She rubbed the sob in Nuala's chest.

"Breathe nice and deep. Slow, breathe slow."

Nuala was exactly where she wanted to be, but it struck her as banal. Her life had always been more of a struggle than Artemisia's and she couldn't resist struggling now.

"They fired me, Artemisia. Just like that. Oh, they offered me a curator's job, but they knew I wouldn't take it. After all these years, they dumped me. That bitch, Modthryth, she engineered it. Said I was alienating the public. Said I was elitist."

"Mode . . ."

"That's what I call her. You know, the Queen Monster in *Beowulf.* She's the chairman of the friends of the museum. The moneybags."

"Have I met her, Nuala?"

"No, I don't think you have. Her name is Gudrun Kierstadt."

Ootwaert's Hoe

If there is anything of Salomé in a woman, Bo believes something hapless in him will call it out. He's the ideal witness to a woman's bad behavior. And that's why chagrin rises like vomit to his mouth when he stands on the ridge overlooking the south plat of the cemetery one September dawn and sees Wraithe, her bronze hair on fire, dancing naked among the stones. He kneels in a triad of arbor vitae. Too fast to be a pavane, too romantic to be modern, her choreography is perfect. She has done it often. When she's finished she sits cross-legged before the lichened stone cross of Flossie Wattrous de Graaf, 1899 to 1928, pours something from a battered decanter into a glass, sips and enters upon a conversation, speaking animatedly, nodding when addressed, gesticulating. Then she rises, picks up a towel, drapes it over her right shoulder and knots it loosely above her opposite hip, and departs, talking to her companion.

A priest elevating the sacred host at mass might as well be a porter compared to the sacred and feral scene he has witnessed. His left leg feels reinforced by a rod when he tries to rise. He shivers and is unamused. Wraithe has the kind of body his mother, Ulrike, paints. Capable like a dolphin's, not lithe. He can't even begin to address the companionability of what he saw, not until his unwitting blood sets. Then he gets up and draws closer, taking cover behind more arbor vitae. If the girl were beautiful, would it be trite? If she were not, would it be compelling? Wraithe doesn't wish to be beautiful, but she can't banish her looks.

He has studied the gravestones here. He's noticed the cross marking where Flossie Wattrous de Graaf lies. He goes to it now and is unable to shake the odd sense that Flossie isn't there, has left with Wraithe. The two Dutch women have gone hand-in-hand for a walk in the dripping wood. A sense of emptiness envelops him. He walks over to Peter Hammer's stone next to Flossie. Here there's no emptiness. Peter Hammer lies there at his feet. He walks back to Flossie's stone and once again he feels bereft.

He makes inquiries about Wraithe. She appeared six years ago. The town board discussed her. The county human services department was consulted. The police declared her harmless, but pressure for her removal built until Police Chief Evan Sanders stood up before the town board and said, "If you're going to get rid of her, why not the junkies?" She at least was sober, if mad. But she continues to have her detractors—cluckers, Sanders calls them—because she's indigent. So are the longhairs on the village green, and near to indigence most of the artists, writers and musicians. The young cops are offended by her enemies. Why pick on her in a town of authorized loonies? These pony-tailed cops are a far cry from the high-school bullies he remembers from childhood. He takes to leaving food in the crook of her oak. He wraps it in plastic bags stowed in a waterproof backpack from the store. He leaves her some silverware in deference to her obvious cultivation. He watches from his evergreen blind as she sits at various stones, eating ceremoniously, chatting, feeding cats, squirrels and birds. This gives him more pleasure than anything since he at age eight filched food from the boarding school pantry and took it to eat in his bullbriar hideout, talking earnestly with his invisible companion and advisor, Amir. This girl reminds him of that nameless bullbriar boy and his friend Amir. God knows he needed a friend in that genteel hell. Yes, and God gave him a stepfather, Sandro, and now Sandro is gone like everyone else on this hill, except for Wraithe and maybe himself—and Flossie.

The autistic need to control their environment, to touch the world only on their terms, these matters he understands. He and Wraithe have broken down on their own terms and must mend in the same way. He touches the jagged scars in his head. The only touch he ever trusted was that of Navy doctors and nurses. How can you yearn for touch and yet not wish to be touched? Bo knows.

So compulsive is his doodling, as he calls it, he'd hardly miss a notebook and he doesn't miss one of the sketchbooks he leaves in his blind on the hill. When he was young his doodling consisted of catenaries resembling comet tails, scimitars, contrails. Not surprising in a merchant marine navigator familiar with great circles, but he'd probably agree if it were pointed out to him that these early doodads were redolent of the Russian constructivists. He might even have agreed they derived of his need to stand clear of people. But his many visits to the Netherlands—he knows every buoy and bell and light in the Nieuwe Maas—drew him inevitably to traditional draftsmanship. He spent many hours sketching in the Stedelijk Museum in Amsterdam. He has no idea to this day his work has been admired by talented peers looking over his shoulder in museums around the world. He's devoid of aspiration. He merely wishes he could draw. He can't think of a more enviable skill. He wonders from time to time if he'd have nerve enough to enroll in art classes, but these reveries are always burgled by remembering the day he showed Ulrike some drawings when he was fourteen. "Oh dear, I'm afraid you're a klutz. But it's all right, maybe God has given you other skills."

With no particular thought in his head, except perhaps for a New Jersey lawyer who seems to be diddling Ulrike out of some of her late husband Hart's stock, he carries egg salad up the hill one morning to find Wraithe bejeweled with six or seven rectangular plaques that catch the sun as they turn in a light breeze. They're clear plastic sandwiches with holes drilled at one end so they can be worn as pendants. He's seen art on paper sandwiched this way. Wraithe turns slowly like a dervish in a trance. Then a piece of paper falls from one of the plaques. She doesn't see it. Her eyes are closed. He picks it up. Others have seen his drawings, but no one honored him with an exhibition, especially not on a crystalline morning in a cemetery. Wraithe moves away, down a gentle slope towards the della Robbia, wearing the contents of his lost notebook. He sets his plastic bowl of egg salad and rolls in the crook of her tree and grins broadly with an inspiration. He takes out a little note pad and writes:

I'm quite enamored of your drawings. Please call me.
Clement Greenberg.

He adds Ulrike's phone number. Not that he can imagine the famous critic being enamored of anything that doesn't affirm his presuppositions. He puts his note and the fallen sketch into the backpack and leaves.

That night, as he sets out on his patrol, Wraithe breaks off her conversation with some shamanic drummers to shake her tambourine at him from across the street. He's already passed her when he realizes she's given him a smile certain artists would foreshorten their lives to paint—a girl he's never seen smile.

They intrude on each other's privacy, spy each other out, and yet hardly speak.

Two days later she introduces him to Theodora Wattrous de Graaf, 1884 to 1926. Will-o'-the-wisps wink around Braithwaite's shrine as they sit at Theodora's stone.

"She killed her husband because he was molesting Flossie, their daughter. Then they found Theodora guilty and killed her. She would like you to draw her and Flossie."

"How did Flossie die?"

"You'll see."

"You talk to the others, Wraithe?"

"Some of them." She adds, "You can. Kurt Meissner over there—he was famous, you know—says you're wonderful. He'll help you if you let him."

Wonderful? He shivers in the critical acclaim. He knows the sculptor Meissner's work and admires it.

"I have very strong feelings about bending children out of shape. My feelings might get in the way."

"Flossie knows that. She told me she'd like to be your lover. She's very pretty. She made a bad marriage. She was very unhappy. She died of sorrow."

"Any marriage would've been tough, don't you think."

Wraithe looks solemnly at him until he sees she apprehended before he did that they are, all of them, children of abuse. Then she turns towards Flossie and says, "She says that's true."

He follows her gaze, hoping to see Flossie. "Flossie can't be my lover now, can she?"

"I'll show you how."

"That would be a ménage à trois," he says and smiles.

Wraithe's eyes smile, but not her mouth. "Oh no, I'm like a concierge."

If your life has been in the hands of an unwilling parent, you probably either babble to fill the void, which you fear is disapproval, or you emulate the parent. Early on he babbled, but when his stepfather Sandro, appreciating that Ulrike had nothing to say, and pursuing his own mythology about the demeanor appropriate to a Saracen—Bo being Arab on his father's side— began to muffle the boy's mouth with a huge hand and a wry expression, Bo launched upon his lifelong compulsion towards silence. More than any other gesture, he remembers Sandro's and even now feels the love in it.

He sits and waits.

"Flossie never wanted any man to touch her. That's why she wants you to draw her naked."

Does this make sense? He shakes off the question. What does make sense? It's not his ignorance of how to draw Flossie— perhaps like a forensic artist he can draw her from Wraithe's mind—it's her use of the word naked that possesses him. Or is it Flossie's?

"I've never sketched a nude."

"Just sit and wait. You'll see her."

He fetches chalk, charcoals and pencils and sets them out on the grass. He opens a sketchbook and shuts his eyes. He feels the sun climb his back, breathe on his neck and overflow onto Flossie's cross. At first he's conscious of Wraithe's presence, but by the time his hand moves he's unaware of her. Within the hour he has drawn a tall, angular woman in her early thirties. Her long face is unutterably sad. She wears a transparent calf-length dress. Her neck rises like a lily stem from ruffled lace. He has used chalk and charcoal, not opening his eyes to tell their colors. She reminds him of someone, but he can't remember. He finds he's drawn her with blue chalk and charcoal. The line delineating her lips from adjacent flesh is as sensual as a Mongol bow. He knows from experience this delineation is telling, one of those details on which a drawing, but not necessarily a painting, depends. Her eyes stare straight at him, an effect he doesn't believe he could have gotten if his own had been open. They disturb him. They belong to someone else he knows, but who? She is blonde. He can tell that as clearly as you can in some old black and white movies, and wisps of her hair stand in the air. She has the prominent nose of that memorable Dutch girl at the church fair, and he imagines her skating on the Rondout, hands in a beaver muff, easily taken for haughty if you did not savor the honesty of her face.

He's drowning in nostalgia for this face. He must come home to this face; he has been at home with it. He tries to lift the page, but his hand trembles too much. Flossie Wattrous de Graaf looks straight at him. He shifts the sketchbook one way and then another. Impossibly she keeps on looking at him. Hungry. Wisps of her hair curl at her temples. Her pubic hair is long and silvery. He knows. Her exquisite fingers cover her right nipple, and her other arm extends downward in an elegant curve. But this isn't what he's drawn, it's what he'll go on drawing. He's barely breathing.

I'd give anything to have her. He must say this to Wraithe. But he knows her answer. You have. Have her? Given anything? He turns and finds Wraithe sitting cross-legged behind about five yards off, her eyes closed and nodding. He's concerned for her: isn't this like finding your sister in bed with your lover? He gets up and shows her the drawing.

"Flossie is my dearest friend. I would do anything for her."

He nods gratefully. He can't think of a thing for which he's been more grateful.

"Now you're not entirely among the dead," she says.

He furrows his brow.

"This is death—what you think is life. They've gone on to

live, to reflect, to be everything they couldn't be here. If you draw them, the ones Flossie tells you to draw, they will be your real friends for the rest of your life. Your death, I mean."

"Will Flossie speak to me?"

"When she's ready."

"Do you want this, Wraithe, for Flossie, I mean?"

"Oh no, she's your lover."

A collector of clutter who discards people profligately, Ulrike is unnerved by the stowed and battened ways of her stranger son. She lurches from room to room pursued by death, seizing the humblest item he leaves about, and one morning it's Flossie Wattrous de Graaf. Bo comes upon her in his room. She trembles violently as she holds Flossie's sketch to the sunlight. He's seen men do that when they've picked up hot wires. He turns and leaves.

All that day, under pretense of errand, he searches the pictorial archives of the Quarry County Historical Society. In two hours he's found de Graafs and Wattrouses. Indeed their patronymic connections look like a road map of the county. He leaves off to amuse himself by leafing through the foxed pages of the defunct *Quarry Telegraph*. Please! he says aloud when he spots Flossie de Graaf, her left arm above her head, holding the lintel of an arbor:

Miss Flossie Wattrous de Graaf, valedictorian of the class of 1909, Clearwater Women's College.

He'll always wonder why he said that word. Please stop this? Please let me wake up?

It's the young woman he's drawn, beyond any possible doubt. Younger, fragrant: the scent of lilac rises from the browning page. His breath comes hard. He feels sweat quit his temples and run down the back of his jaw. Her pose is wrong for its time. It's not demure, it's bravura. What is she looking forward to? She has already suffered grievous wrong. Is this a pose? Her thin, hooked nose is so poignant to him that tears start from his eyes. He drifts in a night sea of intimacy and loss. He's swamped by his urgent need to give everything that has ever caused him to wonder to this girl. His desire for that and for her chokes him.

99

It takes all the charm he can muster to persuade the tidy archivist to let him copy the crumbling page.

His bones hurt when he compares the newsprint image to his sketch: the suppleness, the fey disorder of her hair, the ghostliness of her eyes all match impeccably. Eyes are often shadowed in old photographs, especially in newsprint reproductions, but Flossie's are just as he drew them. Few men would be themselves in that gaze. Right on, Flossie, he thinks. She was—is—a towhead. The hair of her forearms and thighs—and her buttocks—to the eyes of a lover must have looked like winter wheat in Alberta. He imagines himself the sun drowning in her navel. If she weren't so alive to him, he'd give up to desperate mourning.

Dream by dream, Flossie appears to him. By day he pits his confusion against a growing sense of fulfillment. He has three sketchbooks filled with her images. The first book is conventional. He's studying her face and torso. The next two books are different. They startle him when he's finished. He's pictured her riding her bike, parking it, undressing at the brook, sleeping, preparing vegetables, gardening in front of a big stone house. That's it, the house. He goes into Bluestone and digs out old real estate books, the kind in which they used to put drawings of famous properties in bound editions. After two days searching in the basement of the county library, he finds it: De Graaf House, Holly Hill, overlooking the Hudson. It shocks him to touch his own hair, he's so electrified by this find.

On his way to the library to find a picture of a bike of her period a compulsion to speak to her seizes him.

"I want to tell you the meaning of the twenty-six parts of my bicycle brake, Flossie. I had them all laid out on the floor of the garage so I'd remember how to reassemble them. I was oiling them, trying to see how they worked together. It was a wonderful game. I was lost in it. I was eleven years old. Ulrike came in and got hysterical. She was so mad she started to throw tools around. I had a pretty logical mind, so I started to worry that if she mixed up the way I laid out the brake disks and other parts I wouldn't know how to put the bike back together. Then she started hitting me with a grass whip. I had the kind of mind that wondered why the grass whip, why not a broom or the bike's fender. So while I fended her off I chuckled inside me because I knew how blunt the damn thing was. But do you know why she was pissed? No, not pissed. Panicked. It was because she saw her whole summer going down the tube. Jesus, it's taken me forty-one years to figure it out. It wasn't a metaphysical problem. It wasn't psychological. It was practical. It wouldn't have occurred to me that gods worry about logistics. Only little jerk-offs like me did. See, everything depended on me, this eleven-year-old kid. I did all the shopping, everything. On that used bike. The whole operation depended on me all summer long, and I didn't get it. The only exception was the booze. Sandro brought that on the bus every Saturday morning, because it was so important. She kept hitting me with that grass whip until she realized it wasn't doing much good. Then she snatched the bike chain and lashed it around my head and pulled. It was like a chain wrench. It nearly tore my face off. I had to kick her. She hurt me so bad I could hardly think straight to put the bike together again. Blood kept getting in my eyes and I was shivering. When I finally got the bike together and working I had three brake disks left. I still don't know why, but I put them in Ulrike's jewelry box. They're probably still there. She keeps everything she buys, even food."

Snot and bitterness explode from him. He weeps until he retches and has to stop and hide under some willows near the library. He throws up and is so startled by it that he starts to run. When he stops he looks at Flossie's picture again and says, "Nothing's as lonely as vomiting and eyes are never bluer than when rendered in black and white."

Flossie's look heals him.

"If I ever had a boy I'd tell him what depended on him." He sees agreement take shape in Flossie's eyes and he begins to grope for the shape of a thought—it's more like trying to shape water. Every time he urges his bone-aching desire for Flossie toward regret, contentment settles in his bones. To wish her alive, he begins to think, would be less than this, whatever this is. To suffer, to be battered and betrayed by those you love, those who should have loved you, and then, by main strength, to break the cycle, to refuse to repeat the crime, is not to free yourself of ghosts but to be one, to live among them, and then at last to see that many whom you had supposed to live are neither dead nor alive. The dead are not lost. Can the lost die?

"Is this true, Flossie?"

His hand skips and races until Flossie's eyes light and she smiles.

"Do only the discontented haunt, Flossie? No, I think not."

The most difficult thing he's ever learned to do is wait until the truth of something catches up with his gut. No truth given or earned is of any use until then.

So now his childhood knowledge of the cemetery as a resting place mends the broken circuit of his life: he can be, he is what that observant boy was, and this he owes to a mad girl who lives in a tree.

"No, this I owe to me, dear, dearest Flossie Wattrous de Graaf."

His desires clamor. He can't stop drawing her. He can't see, it's veiled to him, that he's used color, not much, blue at first, then a few others. He wants to desecrate this place with his doubts, but deference prevails. It's a done deal. He must go on drawing her until something happens. This man who has never been afflicted by the impendingness of things waits breathlessly.

Flossie Wattrous de Graaf sleeps beside Theodora, her protecting mother. Where will he sleep? Not at Woodlawn. No, he wouldn't rest well there. He and Sandro did not come to a good parting. Artists Hill? With Hart and Ulrike? That Flossie is there too troubles him, and he walks faster to get away from his thought.

He now knows that Evert de Graaf, Flossie's father, was a highly respected judge. Theodora Wattrous graduated from Vassar with a degree in biology. Why were they buried on Artists Hill in Echo Tarn and not in Bluestone overlooking the Hudson? He'd found the Honorable Evert de Graaf's resting place. It was a family mausoleum in Bluestone.

The microfilmed records of *The Bluestone Patriot* reveal little. Flossie is married to Jonathan Ross Waverley when Theodora shoots Evert. Had she just discovered the molestations? Could they possibly have continued after the marriage? Flossie has no children, and she's buried eight miles away under her maiden name. She died only two years after her mother was executed for a murder the reporter calls cold-blooded.

He searches the records of the Dutch Reformed Church. Evert is accorded the usual enrollment. Theodora and Flossie are banished.

He stuffs a small sketchbook into his jacket pocket and takes up his usual midnight watch in front of the hotel. The moon unrolls a silver carpet across Quarry Road to Artists Hill. He gets up and follows it like a dowser, not knowing where it will lead. It leads him to the half buried bluestone memorial to Kurt Meissner. Wraithe says you think I have work to do up here, he tells Meissner. Lead the way. He takes out his sketchbook and a pencil.

Captain Martin Shellenbarger, killed in the Ardennes in The Great War, materializes as he draws. He's a thin-faced young man, not unlike the poet Arthur Rimbaud when he arrived in Paris to ruin Paul Verlaine. Martin Shellenbarger is somewhat walleyed, but his one steady eye is clear and penetrating.

He turns a page and begins to draw Elaine Witte, who died while he was a boy hereabouts. She's oval-faced, eyes long and wary, buxom and lovely.

The moon offers enough light to sketch seven more faces.

He can't find photographs of all of them in the Echo Tarn library or in Bluestone, but when he finds Martin Shellenbarger and Elaine Witte his fingers tremble so violently that he can't turn pages. Martin stands beside a racing scull with three other young men at Yale University. They've just won a race. His hair falls down over his bad eye and he looks straight into the lens just as Bo drew him. Elaine is running after a badminton shuttlecock. The camera has caught the sunlight in her eyes. She is the woman she becomes in Bo's sketch. Four other photographs match his graveside drawings. His heart hurts. His mouth is parched.

To what purpose am I able to draw the dead? What kind of gift is it? Who owns it? Me, Wraithe, Kurt Meissner, Flossie?

He draws for several days but makes no further effort to authenticate his drawings.

He walks every which way and winds up always in the cemetery. He's filled five sketchpads with the residents of Artists Hill. The October sun stands bolt red threatening the damp sleep of the Catskills until the darkness opens. He rises because he hears the sun thundering like sheet metal. He sits in the back of Hart's cottage watching the sun lift out of the Hudson, sore and demanding. He draws the tree line, a doe nibbling elderberry, the gravel pile. Then one day he walks down to Gaia's Art Supply and buys dry colors, at first chalks, then crayons. Finally he buys that most unruly of media, watercolor.

He's painting Flossie on the hill when Ulrike Theiss dies of a massive stroke.

Bo thinks of Anders Ootwaert's tools. Would they still be in the little shed in the woods beside the old cottage Sandro bought in 1945? If so, he wants them.

In the shed, as he pulls the old farmer's tools out from behind broken mirrors, sashes and bedsteads, he thinks of Rudyard Kipling's poem, *If*. Lottie Donovan at boarding school made him memorize it after Johnny McKewn gave him a shiner. He memorized it and then trudged down to the McKewns' Kozy Korner tavern and asked Mr. McKewn if he could see Johnny. Johnny, yer friend from the school is here, Mr. McKewn called to his son. Johnny appeared smirking and Bo decked him. Just like that. Then he stood there waiting for the boy to get up. That'll be enough, Mr. McKewn said, and it was. Except for *If*. Two lines scull in from the mist:

> *[If you can] watch the things you gave your life to, broken,*
> *And stoop and build 'em up with worn-out tools...*

What had he given his heart to? Nothing. And yet now he can see that he gave his heart to be loved by Ulrike. He stoops and picks up Ootwaert's tools. He notices some words scorched into the haft of the hoe: *Whatever you set your heart on becomes a mirage.*

The wind rattles the poplars. Chipmunks scamper in and out of their stone-fence dens. The huge oak he climbed as a boy to see the town two miles away complains arthritically in the wind. What has become a mirage? A red-shouldered hawk stoops. He set his heart on Ulrike liking him, if not when he was young, then in their old age. Not love, complicated and unreliable, but liking. He takes the measure and weight of Anders Ootwaert's hoe as if it were a weapon, and he nods.

The wind rattles the poplars. Chipmunks scamper in and out of their stone-fence dens. The huge oak he climbed as a boy to see the town two miles away complains arthritically in the wind. What has become a mirage? A red-shouldered hawk stoops. He set his heart on Ulrike liking him, if not when he was young, then in their old age. Not love, complicated and unreliable, but liking. He takes the measure and weight of Anders Ootwaert's hoe as if it were a weapon, and he nods.

Gatecrasher

I remember my first faceted bottle of Waterman's ink. My future shimmered on ink's horizon when I looked into it. To hint at my age, it was before the vulgar ballpoint, before I discovered that words dart out from under their assigned meanings. One ignores this at peril, as I ignored my distrust of the word marriage.

I've been called a grande dame. Some fool magazine called me the *doyenne royale* of philanthropists. But I know what I am. I'm a trickster, a gamester of surpassing skill and grace, and this is why I'm sitting in the hauteur of my old age writing a book the bloodless bookies who run the publishing industry won't want to touch because it concerns goodness, which is for them a how-to issue.

When certain people enter your life, if they seem to bring with them a new and better order of things, you don't notice at first that they smell a bit ripe. Insider traders, that's what they are. They're going to let you in on something good. They're a kind of flatulence. Everyone else is less urgent. They encourage you to expect everything will change. When it does (it always does), you're missing a kidney or something.

With the advent of Ariel Rennie I began to search for what might be missing. I knew the Rennies of Manhattan, Southampton, Antibes. She didn't belong to them. But suddenly she belonged to us, our circle, although none of us seemed to know how. She simply appeared at our Christmas Eve party two years ago. Then at receptions, openings, formal dinners, soirées in country estates.

Of all the friendships—enchantments, really—that Ariel made under my feral nose the one with Alicia Dougherty interested me most. Alicia is on one hand gracious and generous and on the other hand a termagant furioso. Yet Ariel attended her like an aide-de-camp.

Only once—quite late in our life together—have I made Andrew laugh. We stood in the driveway of our summer home in Rhinebeck last September watching guests arrive for a party and I cried out, "Oh here comes Alicia Dougherty with her starling-daffy walk and her calumny of crows." I didn't even bother to look at him. I never do. But that night when the poor man offered a toast his eyes fell on Alicia and his words tumulted naughtily into his glass.

Alicia's attachment to Ariel Rennie confirmed me in my suspicion that Ariel was a soldier of the dark, a Renaissance magic term that sticks in my mind, as terms tend to do, for I am an encyclopedist. Or, rather, because I've never had to earn a living, I am an historian of the making of encyclopedias, which means I'm more comfortable in Sumer than Easthampton. This should have endeared me to Ariel. Historians favor interlopers—they must—because they're the wheels of progress. Ariel could pilfer objets d'art or their husbands; she could case art collections or wrest insider information. But what interested me was her style. No, that's not quite what I wish to say—not her style but the dangerousness of her silences, their glamor.

"What do you make of Ariel Rennie?" I asked Alicia when I had her over for cocktails.

It's funny how you can rub shoulders with somebody for years and think you know them and then in an instant watch all your assumptions plop like mousse in your lap. I watched Alicia's eyes glow like sundown on her shoulders' horizon as she poised her answer. I felt like running into the street.

"The fact that her beauty causes facial tics in all but the most predatory men and least narcissistic women suits her well and ultimately, I think, it inspires her secret religious life."

Was this Alicia Doughery? She sounded like me, speaking to peers in a mahoganied room punctuated by green lampshades. It was exquisite. I took away her glass. It was my practice to snocker Alicia as quickly as possible, but now I wanted to hear more.

"Some beautiful women," she said, "find the touch of men, to say nothing of their manner, wholly unequal to their own. I believe Ariel finds the touch of others distracting, disaffecting perhaps."

My facile tongue recoiled in its lair and wouldn't come out.

"Her life is Paulist, its contemplation Cistercian. It's perfect, you see, for a gatecrasher."

Alicia rose in triumph, glanced down at the rubble of my opinions and decamped.

By Thanksgiving I was stalking Ariel, but she was young and agile, and she was not in the *Social Register*. I hired Timothy Blackwell and Associates, respected ferrets who could audit books as well as shadow miscreants. The bills and reports arrived regularly. Information did not. They followed her on March 19th from Clarinda Holmes's party for the empty-headed author James Winesap. She got into a car driven by Dora Lewin and they went to Dora's apartment on Jane Street in the Village. That was Sunday night. Tuesday morning a Blackwell operative found it freshly painted and vacant. The landlord said Harris Kaschembahr, the tenant, had been evicted a month earlier. He never heard of Dora Lewin. Why hadn't that fool Blackwell sent a man there Monday?

Three weeks later Blackwell himself tailed Ariel from a reception up the Henry Hudson Parkway, over the Tappan Zee Bridge, and past Newburgh, only to lose her in a ground fog in the Rondout Valley. But he had the license number of her silver Camry, he wrote apologetically. A week later he reported that New York State never issued such a plate, but it would be a Woodstock plate if it had been issued and one never knows about Woodstock, ha, ha, ha. "I do not pay you for a few yuks, Mr. Blackwell," I told his answering machine. Three weeks messing about Woodstock failed to turn up Ariel or her car, but Blackwell was able to give a good account of a few restaurants.

Blackwell and his gang of gourmands were still dining out on me when we gave an old-fashioned ball just before Christmas to raise money for the Kaatsbaan International Dance Center. We could be sure of competent dancing. I said I was a trickster, didn't I? Well, one of my tricks, a very successful one, is to seem to appear everywhere for about an hour, touching arms, winking, making everyone comfortable, and then to disappear. That's all hostesses are good for, an hour or so; after that they're baggage. My habit is to wander about upstairs. By the time guests leave, I'm refreshed enough to convince them they'll be missed. I grew up in this house. I owe much of my reputation as confidante to its construction. I know which registers and ducts carry sound and from where. The register under a window in the upstairs library confided this piece of intelligence to me the night of the ball:

"Children are magi, Andrew," Ariel was saying, "and at all costs society tries to knock it out of them. Anyone who finds a child's circle of pebbles in a wood or a place where a child has buried a sparrow knows it's holy ground. It's not like finding a yellow plastic pail."

Wouldn't the old goat say anything he could conjure to please the lovely Ariel? His back would be to the fireplace in his study. I imagined her standing behind him, leaning on the mantelpiece. The three of us listened to the logs crackle. Andrew never felt compelled to speak. It was his loveliest trait. He listened with his eyes. Everyone always seems to have Andrew's attention. It makes life with him bearable. But I thought he was abusing the privilege.

"I myself belong to the predator class, Ariel," he said at last. He would be swinging his wheelchair around to face her. I was overwhelmed with a sense of myself as eavesdropper. "We prey not as much on the desperate poor," he continued, "as the pathetically hopeful middle class. They have more money, you see. We do so in the name of competition, the global economy, whatever sounds convincing, but our aim, as it has always been, is to transfer wealth to the Cayman Islands where the do-gooders can't lay their undeserving hands on it. The predator class stage-manages the social debate. Rather operatically, I think. There's talk of inflation, the need to compete for overseas markets, downsizing to raise investment capital—you know the riff, I'm sure—but there is never any talk about obscene profits or whether these profits go into development or investors' pockets."

"I see that you see, Andrew, and that you have resigned from the predator class."

"I have resigned from everything. But I would like to see the circle of pebbles, Ariel, to see it and revere it."

I choked on my olive in remorse. The house in which I had lived my entire life was being strange and untrustworthy. Something like love poked through my flesh like a broken rib.

I drifted around upstairs like a dowser, touching photographs and imperfections in window panes—I saw in them that I was the ghost of the house. But why? There was nothing here I wanted. Nothing had happened to hold me. Nothing. Isn't that why ghosts haunt, because something, someone holds them? I would watch Andrew leave and then I would leave. Andrew whom it seems I never knew.

He is a great contraption of a man, his body sectored by casting seams. Our mating was a technological feat. His face looks as if it had been bolted by a tinsmith and always struck me as knightly for that reason. Making our children was like bustling in a laboratory, collegial, proficient. Once we had nothing more to make, we gravitated to our own bedrooms and our private lives.

My father was a great rarity of our kind. He would have rather supported a drunken artist in Paris for a son-in-law, as long as the fellow had talent, than a fellow mercantile banker, nor did Andrew Stilwell's pedigree impress him. Pedigrees have to do with the achievements of predecessors, and my father had seen enough of the world to know that good genes are at best an easily squandered head start. So he insisted that Andrew should have none of my wealth. It was sufficient help, he said, for others to smell it.

"You will forgive me for this, Maddie," my father had said.

"Why should I have to?" I said. There was nothing to forgive. I didn't know until he was dying that my taciturn father took me to mean that I didn't think I ever would forgive him. So we had a tearful reunion on his deathbed.

Andrew did very well on the scent of my money. I did even better, so I'm far wealthier than he is, but he's wealthy enough.

I went downstairs and stood under the atrium, my hand resting on the newel cap, listening to the orchestra of glasses, the bubbling of conversation and laughter. Ariel came out of Andrew's study. She stood listening to the choreographed gaiety coming from the ball as if she had done it a thousand times. Then, with her hands behind her, she closed the sliding doors. She looked at me and smiled and I believed that she knew everything that I ever would think. "Shush," she said, inclining her head toward the hubbub and crossing her lips with her forefinger, "they're sleeping." Then she was in the doorway and left. As I watched the snow enfold her in a reverie of egrets' wings I had the silly notion none of us would see her again.

An Arcane Casting Mind

Once you've seen certain faces, nothing's imaginable without them. For these faces stars sing, God perseveres. But who knows this?

Empathic lock picks, illuminati of the fey, that's who.

Araby Dunnock earned this knowledge casting film actors as people she knew, people who grew and changed in her imagination. She hadn't examined this habit, so she didn't realize it was limited to people she liked. All her favorite people sooner or later acquired these doppelgangers. Sometimes the more astute felt not quite themselves around Araby.

In time she bent her arcane casting mind to her favorite books. Laurie Colwin and Robertson Davies proved unusually collaborative.

We might have gotten along with Daumier and Nast and Goya, of course, but it took the March of Time and the movies to properly people the language. How easy it became to define pomposity once we saw Benito Mussolini's balcony act. How could we improve on scowl without the Ayatollah Khomeini? And should you want to describe a wicked wolfish smile without indulging in caricature you'd be at a loss but for the inspired disposition of the actress Emma Thompson's teeth.

Other faces are dispensable, and that's too bad, but it's the way things are. It's probably a mixed blessing, anyway, to have one of those cosmically important faces, because so many of us can't bear to be loved or hated.

Araby Dunnock's casting directorate was probably born the day she studied a picture of the British traitor Kim Philby in *The New York Times.* She knew Richard Basehart was born to play him. Unhappily they both died without benefit of Araby's genius.

She didn't know why she hadn't become a casting director with CSA at the end of her name, but it didn't bother her once she recognized that most producers and directors don't let casting directors get in the way of a big name, however inappropriate its bearer to the part. If she were going to be a casting director, she'd have to be boss.

Besides, once she told a producer that Jurgen Prochnow and Dominique Sanda belonged to the same extraterrestrial landing party—she hadn't decided about Willem Dafoe—the jig would be up, wouldn't it? Her talent was best kept out of Hollywood's hands.

Once Araby cast somebody, it was like casting a horoscope. The right actor for the right friend, then she didn't have to worry about her friend ever again. The ones who worried her were the ones she hadn't found anybody to play. For example, she'd never felt right about any of the Mafia bozos she'd seen portrayed until Robert De Niro cast Chazz Palminteri in *A Bronx Tale*. After that she let the Mafia worry the suits.

Araby had cracked her leg when she was a teenager under the tutelage of George Balanchine. It never healed right, leaving her with a wry limp and her druthers, which were to draw and paint. She thought her limp heroic, rather like The Duke walking film after film in that one-hip-up way of his. And living at Number Two Fifth Avenue made Cooper Union easier to get to than the New York City Ballet. The bodies at Cooper Union, true, were not as rewarding to look at, but they were haunted by ideas, which you couldn't say for most dancers.

Her instructors did their damnedest to induct her into the magisterium of abstract expressionism, but one of them, Irene Rice Pereira, kiboshed their efforts. She tickled Araby's Puritan roots by referring to "all that European angst." Perhaps because she was funny, Pereira, a pure abstractionist, encouraged Araby's instinct to portraiture with a sly tincture of surrealism.

They became pals. Pereira's zone was where mathematics and mysticism flirt. She told Araby all the stories she knew of

114

scientists unable to reconcile the grandeur of creation with randomness. But it was her instructor's demeanor towards men that captivated Araby. Pereira was exquisite, but for all that men gnatted about her pestiferously she had nothing disparaging to say of any of them, nor could Araby learn of a single man her mentor ever wantonly hurt. That is rare to say of any beautiful woman and it informed Araby Dunnock's character.

Born to a diminished but well-tended estate, she thought someday she might launch a gallery career if she ran into a gallery owner she felt like casting. Meanwhile, her career puttered amiably. It started when she was painting the doughty dowager Elizabeth O'Faolain.

"Don't disguise the ropes, dear, I earned them."

"The ropes?"

"Veins, dear. I've had an interesting life, so naturally they stand out. All that blood pumping, you see."

Araby touched up her nose with a sable brush, musing on Elizabeth O'Faolain's comment. When she'd cajoled a sneeze, she stared at her subject in her habitual wild-eyed, antic way. "Oh, lovers! You mean all the lovers."

"Of course, fool. Ye think it was the sherry I was referring to? Lord, what those sticks of sons of mine would say I'd love to know. Patrick? Now, Patrick wouldn't dare open his vile mouth, for all the many doxies he boffed under my nose."

"Were there many?"

"Depends on how many's many. I'll say this, I liked 'em all, even the noodles. Oh yes, dear men, grateful men."

"I'm sure they were."

Araby meant it as a compliment, but her words nettled the old woman who now stared at her icily. "You're one of those bluebloods who'd rather waltz with the antichrist than speak of sex. So I'll not ask you about yours."

"Thank you," Araby said through her teeth.

Their relationship not only withstood this contretemps but prospered. Elizabeth O'Faolain lined up mothers superior, abbots, priors, prioresses and sundry Catholic plutocrats before Araby's easel with the efficiency of a Napoleonic firing squad. In the midst of each job she'd call to prattle. The stiffer Araby retorted, the more wickedly the dowager gossiped.

"How on earth did you deal with Father Hanratty's wattles? You know, the ones he earned ruining acolytes and swilling."

"I made him ruddy."

"Oh, he's ruddy all right! Well, thank God you didn't have to do anything about the qualmish quims of the nuns, dear."

"Can't they be as randy as you?"

"One hopes, but I've found them morose, the lot of them, except for Sister—no, I'll not tell you about her."

Araby reveled in the obstinate disdain for conversational vacuums she'd inherited from her father. It was not her responsibility to fill them and she didn't now.

"Well, we'll keep the sister's story for later, so you'll have something to come see me for," Elizabeth offered. And when Araby wouldn't touch that either, the old woman babbled on. "Do you know how you got your name? I do. Somebody didn't want to be there, wanted instead to be far away in fabled, perfumed Araby."

Araby sighed. "Yes, my mother, Constance. She felt her own name was like watching her feet set in cement."

If Elizabeth O'Faolain jump-started Araby's career, it was the governor, Nelson Rockefeller, who fixed its dangerous course. She saw decency and sorrow in his face. Who could play him? Robert Shaw? No, too much anger kneaded into that jaw. Richard Conte? The governor kept staring at her one evening. She was helping her father host a reception. Compton Dunnock was a corporate lawyer. He was born severe. No one ever dared to give him a nickname. Wherever she took up station she felt the governor watching. Where Constance would have been addled or flattered or both, Araby was bemused. She picked up a tray of champagne flutes and went straight for him. He didn't take a glass, he just looked into her eyes and said gravely, "I like your face." Then he waited. She studied his face carefully. She's going to say, *I like yours,* is what she read in his face. He was immensely relieved when she said, "I rather like it too." They grinned at each other and she departed.

But the governor's remark entranced her. Not because of his good taste. That was renowned. But because he said it. She had a handsome face, albeit a bit austere. An art collector, which the governor famously was, might appreciate it, but that's not why he said it. He said it because he thought it important to say it at that moment. Some twenty minutes later she sallied back into the governor's face. "Would you like me to paint yours?"

"It's been done, Miss Dunnock. What would you look for?"

"What I so plainly see, the sorrow."

"No one will wish to hang it. Do you specialize in paintings that can't be hung?"

"I aspire to—they're the only ones worth painting."

"You are looking at me as if you'd never seen a human soul before."

She lost her nerve. "I didn't mean to be rude."

"Of course you didn't. And you're not rude, you're an artist. And I quite agree with you about paintings. We don't really want to see each other, and artists are very uncouth that way, forcing us to see. I'll tell my secretary you'll be calling, shall I?"

Constance thought it a great coup. Compton felt rather sorry for the governor. Araby thought it a commission beyond bearing.

Over time it got around that Araby Dunnock painted the real you. She painted your karma. She had cachet, but not for the faint-hearted. She was the *portraitiste du jour* for people fitting out within themselves for a journey. She turned some commissions down and abandoned others. Her portraits were focal in epiphanies, divorces, affairs, departures, arrivals and sea changes. She unplugged her telephones. She didn't want to hear from her clients. She was getting frightened.

In this state, descending Fifth Avenue from her studio on Fifteenth and Union Square near Farrar, Straus & Giroux, she bumped into Jean-Hugues Anglade, the French actor who tutored *La Femme Nikita*. Ordinarily she would have been happy to see him, even if he insisted on disguising himself as her cousin Demarest, but not this afternoon, not in her demonic state.

Demarest was in fact neither himself nor the sculpted M. Anglade. Without warning, with a beautiful stranger in tow, her family favorite had been waiting outside her high-rise to waylay her. She was cross as she stared at him over Eighth Street, but M. Anglade's famous gravitas deserves real anger or fascination, and she didn't have the time to sort herself out.

"Demarest, this is a surprise!"

"It's awful, Araby, I know," he said, embracing her. "It calls for indignation."

"Not while you're managing my money, dear." She always handled Demarest as if she were an aunt, to conceal her attraction to him.

"I do apologize, Araby, truly I do. We were doing the Village and I thought, when you weren't home, that we'd meet as you came down from your studio."

"It's not comforting to have one's habits so well charted. Hello, I'm Araby. Of course you know that."

"I do," the girl said, "I'm Lark, Lark Godwin. It's a great pleasure. Demmy has told me so much about you."

This greeting struck Araby as professional. Lark Godwin was drop-dead beautiful. She did not seem to chafe under Araby's scrutiny. She was probably not the sort of blind beauty who'd hike her shoulders and get huffy about being appreciated. On the contrary, she probably smiled beneficently at her admirers. Araby could tell that and liked it.

It boded ill, to Araby, that Demarest had doffed his patrician manners to make this visit. She did not think it innocent, and she was right. He wanted her to paint Lark Godwin. They were affianced, he explained, and he wanted to have her portrait before she looked married.

"In the wild, so to speak?" Araby said helpfully. Too helpfully, because she was astounded. Jean-Hugues Anglade pleading? Jean-Hugues Anglade suggesting that marriage to him might exact a toll. What in hell is going on? Demmy? A man with a face like that allowing himself to be called Demmy? But she just stared. The more she stared the more her cousin squirmed. Until it came to Araby that he was the wrong person to examine.

By this time they had ascended to her balconied apartment overlooking Eighth Street. She made tea to dilute her dismay. This commission could have been accomplished by telephone. But, come to think of it, Lark did have a right to examine the artist. She raised her gaze to Lark Godwin. Lark was looking at Demarest as if he'd embarrassed her. Had he? Then she turned a conspiratorial look at Araby. Men are irredeemably silly, aren't they? her look said. But Araby was having none of it. Demarest had never been silly, until now.

This was not a commission she could turn down. Demarest had always been kind, teaching her to sail, making sure boys treated her properly, caring for her trust, things like that.

The girl had the kind of beauty that disturbs one's sense of order. It could not leave you alone, nor you it. Araby got it right immediately. Then she noticed she'd unerringly painted the backdrop bloody red. Was it the banshee raven hair that invited it? The long blue eyes? The pale skin? The red engulfed and shook the girl. One day while Araby quarreled with herself the girl obligingly turned so that Araby might notice that her nose stooped to meet her pointed chin in the classic crescent caricature of a witch.

She knew then she should abandon the portrait, but Demarest would take it badly. It would sour the girl to his dotty family. So, fretting and pricking a malign mote into the girl's eye, she finished it.

Greeted with oohs and ahs, carried off like booty, it haunted Araby and kept on haunting as disquieting news of Demarest and his wife trickled in: sudden crib death of their baby girl, Demarest diagnosed as having multiple sclerosis, Lark frequently a conspicuous absentee. When Araby visited them in East Hampton he looked drained. Lark looked whetted, as if the world were indeed her namesake. Her conversation, such as it was without a script, was often sarcastic, therefore vulgar.

119

Standing before her portrait one evening as they waited for her to return from work, Araby said, "I wish I hadn't painted her." She expected Demarest to protest or to reassure her. Instead, he poured himself a cognac and asked, "Did you consider her profile when you were painting her?"

She poured herself one. When she turned to his inquiry he was smiling. "Yes, I noticed." She patrolled the study, fondling his books. She had miscast him. That was the problem. Then she swung around. "Demarest, you look rather like Sting, do you know him?"

"*Stormy Monday.* Film noir. It's extremely stylish. I liked his demeanor, it was stoic, but wasn't fatalistic. His enemies underestimated him."

He shared her love of films. She felt herself poised to do what Nelson Rockefeller had adjured her to do. "Well, yes, Demarest, you are rather like him in that role, I see that. Harried, but far from beaten, even a little dangerous."

Now he grounded to his books. She stared at his back while he considered. The house ticked with clocks. His shoulders shook. She'd never seen a Dunnock or a Findlayson adult cry. She was going to console him when she realized he was laughing.

"Demarest?"

"I'm rather tired, Araby, I think I'll just turn in." In the foyer, just before climbing the stairs, he turned and said, "It will be all right, you know that, don't you?"

She nodded.

His wife was in for a stormy Monday one of these days.

The arcane casting mind has odious responsibilities. There would be a Tuesday after stormy Monday.

She wandered about Demarest's study, touching books. Then she went up to her room. As she passed his she noticed the door ajar, so she looked in. He was propped up in bed, a book face down on his breast. He smiled.

How could she signal, given the rationed emotionality of their class, that she had faith he would prevail?

"Good night, Sting," she said.

Return Flight

I know what he detests about me. It is my gray-green uncompromising gaze. My mother's. My father, like all undertakers, looked at people as prospects. Usually I don't give people I unnerve the time of day. But this isn't just any young man, so I hear, it's my son. I feel bad about him. He's tatty. Why is he shorter than me? His father wasn't that short. Maybe he has my hair, too wispy to do anything about, but who can tell, it's so greasy.

I want to shake him, tell him to stop acting like a mongoose, because I'm not a cobra, but I know how shamed you are when your blood leaps up to greet someone your brain can't stand, and I guess my being an old lady confuses him.

All I asked for is a breaker for a one-hundred-and-ten-volt service for this shack I'm renting—and he lectures me about codes and licensed electricians. This is a politically correct town. Once the poets and artists got elected, they adopted every code they could get their hands on. I snap the breaker in his face, he gets into a snit and cowers in a corner behind his computer. A few minutes later he's back, giving this poor mouse hell for bringing me the wrong breaker, which I was about to tell her anyway. Is she his wife? Looks simple enough to be.

Could be he's somebody else's son. I've got some more homework to do. But I do see his father's narrow face and slippery eyes. You had to strain your neck to see what Harry was looking at when you talked to him. He'd stare at the ceiling while we made love, and I had the best boobs in the county, which everybody knew because I played basketball. I could do without a lot, but I couldn't do with Harry not looking anybody in the eye.

Maybe that's his kid's problem too. Leave it to me to cow such a one. I'm lucky I didn't come back here to find a son I'd be attracted to. It might have happened if my genes had done better by him.

I've been going back to his hardware emporium not to watch him get het up about me but to see if that mouse—it's his wife all right—might be nursing a yen to split. She doesn't look it. Guess I didn't either. Big tall open-faced redhead that I was, known around three counties for shoulder-busting hockey and basketball, who'd have thought I'd vanish? Not me.

It happened fast. We were one of those Catskill towns sandbagging against the Borscht Belt. Back in the thirties there were cross burnings. It always beat me why "stinking cowards"— my mother's words—would do such a lovely thing, that's how worldly I was. During the war the volunteer fire department let an empty hotel on the mountain burn to cinders because it was owned by a Jew. Nobody ever said so, but I saw those smirks at firehouse picnics. Poor man who owned the hotel was off fighting in France.

Depending on your outlook, the spire of our Dutch Reformed Church could be praying for deliverance from the artists and writers who discovered the town between the wars—or from the town's tumorous hardness. By the time I came along there was a lot of fear of foreign faces—people from places we'd never heard of, like Armenia, Azerbaijan, Latvia. It was exciting. I loved it. So did my mother. The artists were always making pictures of me. My father figured it meant more people to bury, and some of the artists were good stone-cutters, so we started to have a pretty artsy cemetery. The town was torn between love of hatred and love of money. It opted for a kind of surliness sold as local color.

I put in a year at Bard but found I'd rather skate and shoot hoops. Harry had just inherited his father's store. I was too athletic and vinegary for him, but it struck him as a good match financially. I mistook his shyness for niceness. Teen-age girls are trance walkers. My mother used to say girls should be deep-frozen from sixteen to eighteen. Sure would have saved me some grief.

There was this boy—it was nineteen-forty-four—I saw him everywhere. He belonged to summer people who had no car, so he did their errands on his rickety bike. He was beautiful, fourteen or fifteen. I was nineteen, married about a year, working in that same store over there. I dealt with the customers, especially strangers—they saw Harry's eyes were too close together—so naturally I waited on the boy, which I liked to do because I made him blush. He'd bring in a radio or toaster to be repaired, he'd buy paint, things like that. He had green eyes like mine, only deeper than quarry water, and black hair, and no matter how hard he blushed he'd look back at me just like I looked at him. I'd have to hunch over so my nipples wouldn't look so alert.

It was common practice during the war to cheat summer people and the weirdos, by which we meant the artists and writers, out of ration stamps. You had to be sharp. The ones who knew how many stamps to give you, you couldn't gyp. But the ones like the boy, who just handed you the book of stamps, them you could cheat. Most townspeople passed on the stamps to family and friends, but some sold them. We had what nowadays folks call a convenience store right next to our hardware store and this one day I saw the clerk tear off three times what the boy owed him for sugar. The boy knew, but he sensed the meanness in the town and knew better than to bitch. I walked over to the register, shouldered the clerk to the side and handed his stamps back to the boy. I should have been as smart as the boy and let well enough alone. I saw tears in the boy's eyes and I knew—I've always known such things—they weren't for his hurt feelings, they were for me and the trouble he knew he'd bought me.

This boy always parked his beat-up old bike in our alley, and a week or so later I was wrestling a sack of feed in the storeroom out back when I looked out the window and saw Harry glance back out of his truck and back over the bike. The boy came around the corner from Stuehle's with an ice cream cone in his hand just in time to see. He threw himself at Harry and Harry punched his face. I ran out and beat the shit out of Harry. I had him down on the gravel smashing his face back and forth when the boy jumped on me and started pulling me off. I got up and we hugged each other. I was hot and sweaty and pissed as an addled copperhead. We held each other for dear life. Pretty soon we were both blubbering. Harry started to pick himself up and I kicked his butt. "You little piss ant, I oughtta pinch your ding off," I said.

Then I looked at the bike. It was scrap metal. I went inside, took a brand new Columbia Flyer off the wall and brought it out to the boy. By this time Harry was up and spitting blood and looking like he had a little character for a change. I stuck my finger into his face and said, "You open your mouth, I'll pound you into the ground like a post." Then I scooted the boy off.

It was maybe three days later I caught a ride from an eighteen-wheeler on 9W. And that's all she wrote. Until now.

I waitressed in Nashville, Memphis, Little Rock and lots of watering holes till I had enough money to take flying lessons. Dunno why, just got the notion. I started crop-dusting various places. Wound up about twenty years ago down by Lake Sumner in New Mexico. Bought a little field and air taxi service. Sal is my Apache mechanic and handyman. What I don't do, which isn't much, he does, including, on a good day, my plumbing.

I guess Sal made me come back. He was replacing a Piper's hose. "Damn it, Sal," I said, "when're you gonna learn to do things the white way? If you're gonna replace a hose, replace 'em all."

He grabs my crotch. "You hear yourself say that?"

"No, was it good?"

He squeezes harder. Andy Verplanck pops into my head. Maybe if Sal had kept on squeezing, enough would have popped into my head that I wouldn't have had to come back. I'm not one of those people who every once in a while is stopped in her tracks by the memory of a perfect gesture. But when we graduated from high school Andy went out and spent a fortune on a Bulova watch for me, the kind with a round face clasped by a black cord, and he didn't even want to date me, he just liked me. Some people would be pole-axed by such a memory every time. Not me, not till Sal grabbed the boss's crotch. I thought

Andy did a lovely thing. I thanked him. That's all. But I know people whose lives are blighted by memories, especially if later on things don't go well between them and the person involved. Memories are like rogue cells. People think acting crazy tames them. Mine brought me back here.

As I said, the business of my family has been to bury to the inhabitants of this town. My sister's husband still does. My father, a genteel cadaver, did it for forty years. He was for almost as many years the vice chairman of the local Republicans and fond of saying folks knew better than to vote Democrat because if they did they knew he'd bury them upside down. Some of my girlhood was spent fretting if that meant face down in their coffins or coffins upside down or head down. I had that kind of zany mind. My mother, a Vassar girl whose Dutch ancestors farmed hereabout, was put out with me when I finally brought this conundrum to her. "Foolish girl, your father has a laconic wit, is all."

Maybe the foolish girl inherited enough of his laconic wit to savor collecting the benefits of being dead, dead to this town, anyway. I sure do enjoy people enjoying my death, but I haven't figured out yet what the cover story is. Don't know if I care. What can they say that wouldn't sound like television at two in the afternoon?

Most class reunions are held in plastic dumps out on strip malls or basketball courts, but I've been going to them up on Artists' Hill where the Dutch and the artists and writers sleep rather amiably. Why on earth did Flossie Wattrous die before me? She looked like a peach sundae. Everybody around her acted like a spoon.

And there's Andy. Wonder what kind of life he had. I know a lot of people here, to say nothing of my parents. I pass my sister at the post office. She doesn't recognize me any more than she did when we shared the same bedroom.

I like to sit by the della Robbia at the foot of the hill. It's wreathed by beautiful poison ivy. Twice now I've seen this tall man—about my age—set a bucket down by a big granite slab and start scrubbing.

"Damn birds can't read English," I says to him the other day.

He looks up at me grinning. "Guess he wasn't."

"Wasn't what?"

He points to the epitaph. *Beloved By All Who Knew Him.* "Somebody comes up here and craps on him. Perfect little pooplets."

"Not surprising in this town," I say. "Who was he?"

"My mother's third husband."

"You come up here to scrub your mother's third husband's gravestone?"

He's standing now. Tall as me. "Yeah, it's a dirty job, but somebody's gotta do it."

I laughed so hard I peed. I could tell he enjoyed making me laugh. It seemed kind of conspiratorial, like we'd done it before.

"He was a rascal. I kinda got to like him while he was dying across the road over there. I nursed him. She got loony and he told her to go back to Manhattan so he could die in peace. I was maybe the only one in the world who knew what he meant, so I figured I oughtta stay."

"Rascals are what this town grows best, you know. How many good people you know from here?"

He sloshed his bucket on the beloved. "There was one a long time ago. Worked in the hardware store. Took a powder, I'm told. Best lady in the whole town. Beautiful too."

I had a little trouble ratcheting my gaze up from his grin. When I did I saw his eyes were green, like quarry pools. I knew his gray hair had been black.

Café of the 13th World

The ordinary syzygy of things breaks down. In one of the thirty worlds the café where I sit shimmers and changes. I see that people are not obliged to keep their shapes. I see that I know them in only one of their shapes, the one they keep in politeness to me. They wonder if they can charm me into their circle. They're the same people who staff the usual café. But they live in other worlds at the same time. I see their stories riot behind their words. This cast won't take direction. Seeing pleasure light my face, my favorite waitress points to a sign two busboys are scrubbing. It says Café of the 13th World.

I'm writing this down as a defense against clarity because there are things we can't bear to know. Either I know this or I made it up, I'll never know.

"I urged him to start keeping a journal and that's what he wrote. Schizophrenia, especially paranoid schizophrenia, is virtually untreatable. If you're not going to let me use Zyprexa or Risperdal or some other drug you tie my hands because talk's not going to help this man. Without drugs all we can do is watch him compost."

"Doctor, there's a time when you have to stop talking about what you can't do and start talking about what you can do. What about that don't you understand? Treating this man is a matter of national security. Find the envelope and push it, Doctor."

"Psychiatry is not physics, sir. If I'm going to help him I need to know more about him."

"Damn it, doctor, I don't care if you help him or not—just treat him, he has things in his head we need."

"Then I'm going to have to know something about what went into his head in the first place. You can start with his vita."

"I can't give you that."

"Sir, if you are any indication of how this government is run we are well on our way to becoming a third-world nation."

"What if I were to tell you that if you can put this man back together in some semblance of his former self this nation could start navigating the stars?"

"I'm aware, that is to say, I have some inkling that he's a scientist of some kind."

"That's putting it mildly, doctor. The man holds doctorates in pure mathematics, physics and engineering. There's nobody quite like him on the planet. If you can't fix him we might have to clone him. Does that give you a clue how important he is?"

"He's talking about a café on the thirteenth world, thirteen out of thirty worlds? You're telling me this man is a genius?"

"Genius doesn't even begin to describe him."

"If he keeps on writing in his journal I may find the place where he went off the tracks. Without drugs I have to rely on words. His words. It's as simple as that. Psychiatry is not as advanced as you seem to think it is, sir."

"I'm interested in this man, doctor, because we can be far more advanced than you can imagine."

"In that case you won't mind if I bring in consultants."

"You can't bring anyone in we don't vet, but go ahead and we'll vet them."

"That means no Russians, no Chinese, no Iranians, no North Vietnamese, no Arabs?"

"It means we'll vet them."

"And if . . ."

"We'll kill them."

"If you can't use them you'll kill them?"

"And that's a good argument for you to choose carefully, doctor. You need to put his journal under lock and key. Better yet, bring him a safe and give him the combination. When you take him for a walk or for tests or whatever we'll get into it and photograph the journal."

"Every day?"

"Every day."

"And since we're playing science fiction here, what about the thirteenth world, thirteen out of thirty, does that make sense?"

"I'll have to get back to you on that, doctor. Is it important?"

"Yes, I think it might help me, it might be a start."

She's not god enough to bear what she knows.
She punched me with the palm of her hand and said
it again studying her face in the pupil of my eye.
When you start acting according to what you know
you end up in a place like this with fat Doctor Minorgod here
asking you if you know who you are.
No more than you do, I tell him.
Who is she? We could start there.
I'm running a little test of my own, you know.
Tell me about it.
I'm measuring how long it will take before you and your apparatchiks
cave in to the rule of greed.

"The thirteenth world you were asking about, doctor."

"Yes?"

"Some medieval Arab mathematician and alchemist in Spain postulated it. He said there were thirty worlds of which this is one. The thirteenth world is inhabited by shapeshifters. We're interested in this, doctor, that's all I can say."

"That's all you can say, but you'd like a miracle from me yesterday."

"We're asking you to be a patriot."

"I'm fat Doctor Minorgod."

"Government's full of fat patriots, doctor."

"Carmen, this man is so much smarter than I am and the G-man is so much dumber than either of us that I'm in a terrible fix between them. This patient doesn't live in the same place we do. He doesn't live in the same world."

"Then ask him to help you get a passport to his world."

Efrem Steinmetz stares at his wife with a familiar mix of admiration and frustration. Growing up in South Bronx imbued

129

Carmen Vasquez, his wife, with the conviction that America is getting dumber because its politicians like it that way. As a teacher she thinks it obvious that we'd spend more if we wanted the electorate to know more, if we wanted them to vote. She knows that everything that was made to seem difficult to her was done that way for a purpose, and the purpose was to keep her and her kind from taking charge. Efrem only started to get good as a psychiatrist when he met Carmen. Before that he was book-smart and people-dumb. Carmen knows that math and science often stump girls because so many teachers are pricks. She knows that colleges graduate people—they write the crawls for CNN—who can't spell or parse sentences because the last thing crooks in suits want is a smart voter. Things are the way they are for a reason.

"With schizophrenia the best you can get them to do is go back to where they started, and that's dangerous because the only thing you know about where they started is that it was dark," he said.

"I'm just a teacher, Efrem, but it seems to me in that case you have to encourage your patients to continue their journey. What else can they do? Maybe they're like Columbus. His men thought he was sailing off the face of the earth. He had a crazy hunch he was sailing around it. Maybe he was schizophrenic. Can we be sure he wasn't? Sometimes—please don't be mad at me—I think you shrinks are like Columbus's sailors. You're flat-worlders."

"Well, there were certainly people who called him mad. It would be better if I weren't dealing with an idiot. I don't mean him, I mean Sandy Portman the G-Man."

"Well, unfortunately, Efrem, the voters feel at home with idiots. Has it ever occurred to you that our schools stink because the politicians like them that way?"

"You know, I couldn't find my way home if you weren't such a shining beacon. He calls me the fat Doctor Minorgod. He thinks I don't know my ass from my elbow."

"You don't, Efrem, not where he's concerned, do you? Let him go where he's going. See if he'll give you the privilege of going along. Trust him."

"D'you know what you're saying, Carmen—throw out what I've learned, fly in the face of my betters?"

"Efrem, you're a kike—they expect you to be wily and to play along. I'm a spic, they expected me to get knocked up when I was thirteen and rob a Seven Eleven with my coked-up pimp when I was fifteen. Now if all the kikes and spics and ragheads and slopes and wops and niggers do what *they* expect us to do, where would we be?"

"Well, you know the answer, Carmen."

"I know it, but you don't, Efrem. We'd be where they want us to be. There's an enemy out there, Efrem—you work for him."

"And this has what to do with Marcantonio Whitman?"

Carmen grins like the Cheshire cat.

While CNN baits the nation with word that it's about to divulge why a mother and her thirteen-year-old son spent a week waiting in line for doughnuts, Sandy Portman shifts painfully on a hemorrhoid cushion in his office at an agency so secret its name is known only by the people who work there, the Secretary of Defense, and three people at the White House. He is combing the web for cheap Viagra. He'd gladly face life without it if he could avoid his two o'clock with Vice President Cheney.

The vice president, who regards the Catskills of New York State as foreign molehills, wants to know why thirty million dollars has been poured into a hole on Panther Mountain in Big Indian Valley in the Catskills to excavate a junkyard. About the only comfort Sandy Portman finds in the situation is that the vice president is keenly aware it isn't his money.

The vice president knows that metallurgical analysis shows the junk to contain nickel and other metals in densities unknown on earth. Now the kind of idea that greased Sandy Portman's way to the top lights up a dark knoll in his mind. Tell the vice president, Sandy, how the find on Panther Mountain dovetails with the war on terrorism. Don't tell him it might provide an alternative to fossil fuel. Mr. Vice President, if we can decode the cipher running in that junk it will dwarf the technological advances represented by the locomotive, the automobile, the airplane and the hydrogen bomb. We're Neanderthals compared to the people who made that junk.

The veep will say, What about fossil fuel?

I will say, It will have its place, sir.

He will say, I don't want it to have its place, I want it to be God, have you got that, Portman?

Not only is there nothing to say to make the vice president happy, there's no progress to report. Marcantonio Whitman is pacing his locked-down suite at Johns Hopkins Hospital getting nuttier by the day. And if there's anybody else in the world who can crack those codes Sandy Portman doesn't know about it— not the kind of thing he wants to tell the vice president. Well, never mind the codes, we'll talk about excavation, engineering design, we'll talk about every goddamned thing in the world except that stream of symbols ghosting through the dull black metal in that junk pile up there. Don't tell the vice president that the big foreheads from M.I.T., Cal Tech and Stanford have no clue. Don't tell him the metallurgists can't even scratch that metal. Don't tell him Marcantonio Whitman seems to understand the code and doesn't think his bosses deserve to know what the code means. Don't even tell him Marcantonio exists.

Portman takes a break from his morose thoughts to order Viagra from New Zealand. He opens a safe, takes out a DVD, inserts it and watches the Panther Mountain claptrap drift by. No hard matter on earth is capable of conveying such optical technics. The symbols are abuzz with diacritical marks that change colors. They brighten and fade. Certain symbols enlarge and flash, then resume their former shape and progression right to left. Occasionally they halt and reverse themselves. Sometimes the symbols nod out, then form triangles, circles, vortices, rectangles, polyhedrons. Their acrobatics seem endless, without pattern or interval.

The scientists and linguists are rapt and scared. They wander around the famous meteor crater like lost souls. The density of the magnetite loosens their brains. Their fillings hurt, their eyes wobble in their sockets.

The locals are buying the story that a bunch of geologists from around the world are studying the meteor that strung Esopus Creek like a necklace around the mountain surrounding the crater. The locals lick their chops—the geologists bring money. But sooner or later the story will get out. Then it will have to be debunked, like Roswell. The government's not good at solving problems, but it's good at lying about them.

Lying about Panther Mountain will be a cakewalk. If you can sell a war you can sell a little dig in the Catskills. But how do you sell Dick Cheney on a good reason not to just fill in the hole and move on?

The answer comes with hemorrhoidal zeal. God, you're a genius, Portman. Tell the veep the only company on earth capable of handling this project is Halliburton's Kellogg Brown & Root. He won't hear anything else you say. When in doubt appeal to greed. It's the only sure way to the top. Never mind it's exactly what Marcantonio Whitman is babbling about. He doesn't have to know what real men in real time say to each other in the highest levels of government. Whitman had his chances to get real. He doesn't understand there's nothing like a good cigar and the companionability of practical men. It's too bad. He went wrong somewhere and we'll just have to slap him upside the head and get him to work right for a month or two. After that who cares?

A painful hemorrhoidal twinge snaps him out of his self-congratulatory reverie. How in the hell will I ever convince Halliburton they need Marcantonio Whitman? Hell, they'll just start drilling to Beijing and when they get there they'll sell the Chinese Taiwan and the end of disease. Wake up, Sandy, you don't have to convince Halliburton of anything. They just want the money and you're the wizard who figures out all those clever ways to hide it in the budget. They'll love you, Sandy. They won't niggle. They're real men, their eyes are on the birdie. There's a class of men who serve the men who understand the uses of greed and protect them from too much knowledge. Too much knowledge makes them crazy. They start wars. Sandy Portman belongs to this class. He knew it when he was at Harvard. He didn't have a father who could buy Harvard a library wing. His grandfather didn't excel at rowing, he excelled at hornswoggling drunken Cossacks. So it was Sandy Portman's fate to serve the men who know just what clothes greed wears, just how it talks and behaves in clubs and tennis matches. Serve these men well and a whiff of their privilege will rub off on you. But never take your eye off them, because they're treacherous. Right, grandfather?

He stands up, blows hard on the intake of his cushion, snuffs his computer and goes to lunch. The veep would not be able to grasp how smart Whitman is, and what's the point of upsetting him? In any case, it's best not to talk about people with names like Efrem Steinmetz and Marcantonio Whitman around people with names like Bush and Cheney unless they can design moralizing scams. Yes, a little Viagra from New Zealand, a dab of Preparation H, a four-star lunch, and then go shit the veep. But he will want to know what powered that junk heap into Panther Mountain, Portman. It damn well didn't use fossil fuel to get here. We think they may have teleported the whole thing, Mr. Vice President. Right, they may have teleported it right into Panther Mountain and turned it into a doughnut. Is it radioactive, Portman? No, sir.

He's not going to like anything about this. But maybe the Halliburton schtick can keep him conned until Steinmetz figures out how to fit Whitman's pieces.

"I've given him miles of video so he can study the code, Carmen, but when I ask him if he's had any breakthroughs he just looks at me sympathetically as if I'm the patient. He hasn't written a thing in his journal about it. The videos don't seem to interest him. The people in his head are answering him."

"You have to talk to him about the café of the thirteenth world, Efrem. That's what interests him. Ask him if he thinks they'd serve you in his café."

She watches the taillights of her idea disappear in the dark of her husband's eyes. "I can't do that," he says, "because he doesn't know we're reading his journal."

"You want him to crack a code, to read those symbols. You suggested he keep a journal. You thought he'd write something about Panther Mountain in it. Instead he writes gobbledygook about shapeshifters and the thirteenth of thirty worlds. But maybe he did what you suggested. Maybe he is writing about the code. Maybe while he was up there at Panther Mountain he walked into a café somewhere—there must be villages nearby—and he experienced something he's trying to understand. His brain isn't like yours, that's why you need him. But he won't give you anything without respect, Efrem. Count on it. I know. I grew up in South Bronx. You diss, you lose. That's the deal."

"Yeah, sure, Carmen, that's why the voters think Bush is swell. Get real. They love being dissed. He cuts their federal taxes, their state and local taxes go up ten times as much as the federal taxes, and they think he's the Marlboro Man. Sure, Carmen, it's as simple as not dissing anyone you want something from. In your dreams."

"Well, you can just go on being a schmuck and see where it gets you, Efrem. But I'll tell you one thing, Marcantonio Whitman lives in a better world than you do. Those stupid videos are reminding him that he needs to be there, on Panther Mountain, and that's all they're doing. They're just a strongbox of snapshots. He needs to interact with it. How smart do you have to be to see that?"

"Okay, say his journal is a clue. How can I use the clue if I can't tell him I know about it? I'd have to say the schmucks have tied their shoelaces together."

"Why did they take him off the mountain, Efrem? Why did they bring him to you?"

"They gave him a folding chair and he sat there looking at those symbols and crying. He couldn't stop crying. They asked him what was wrong and he said nothing is obliged to keep its shape. They got excited. Sounded like he was on to something. Then he said they're restoring the pantheon. Well, that didn't sound too promising, but they humored him. Who's restoring the pantheon, Dr. Whitman? We are, he said, with their help.

135

Which pantheon? they asked. The gods, he said. And that's how it went for a day or two, and when they figured he was just going to circumlocute they decided he'd had a psychotic break and brought him to me."

"Under arrest?"

"Well, you can arrest anybody for anything these days."

"Did he have a psychotic break?"

"You can make a good case that Einstein was having one as he worked out the theory of relativity. The more I know about psychoses the more I admire them."

"That's the part of you I admire, Steinmetz. You put that man back in his chair and let him cry his heart out."

Marcantonio Whitman grew up in Watts. He was an indifferent student in high school. He liked basketball only because it was fun jumping around without hitting your head on the ceiling. Whitman was almost seven feet tall, which has its pros and cons. He disguised his boredom as stupidity, and if it hadn't been for his natural proximity to the hoop and passable playing he never would have seen a college classroom. But once he did he transferred from UCLA to Stanford in short order, and after that there wasn't enough mathematical knowledge to challenge him. Still isn't.

He regards Efrem Steinmetz's melancholy face this morning with concern. He likes the man. "Would you like to know the first thing I deciphered, Dr. Steinmetz?"

The delight on Efrem's face almost makes his patient laugh.

"Flu fears, tuna concerns—you know, like the CNN crawl—that's the first thing I saw. In plain English. D'you think they could've gotten here without a sense of humor?"

"The hieroglyphs interact with you then?"

"Post no bills, that's the next thing they said. Look, I've written down what they said." He twirled the dial on his safe and snatched his journal.

"Look, this isn't my shorthand, this is what they said. I know because they repeated it:

—top ten's rule of law / dissent's remaindered / greed rips open the ozone layer / decencies are cooked / statues piss vodka for crooks / bigots bully every people / newspapers abhor news / books abhor ideas / bankers steal / brokers loot / advisors lie / stay tuned / curb your dog / allelujah, what's it to ya? / your call is important to us / all visitors must be announced."

"That's what they said? That's what happened when you cracked the code?"

"I didn't crack anything. Hell, I'm cracked, remember, doc? I sat there scribbling like a maniac and then they give me one of those smiley faces and send me to a café in Phoenicia where I experienced the psychotic break you've been telling me about since I got here. Do you think you can reverse-engineer an intelligence like that?"

"How can they know these things, Dr. Whitman? They were buried in a mountain until the geologists did those test bores."

"I have no idea who or what they are, but I know they know more about us than we do."

"But nobody else has seen anything in English. There isn't a single symbol anybody can recognize."

"It was just before Christmas. I'd begun to cobble together some kind of transcription process. But I was lonely in the midst of all those apparatchiks pushing me around. I missed my books, the things I write on my walls, my park bench, my landlady. Most people don't understand the operations of the mind because they see everything as competition. I was so lonely I just started talking, like you would to a teddy bear or a dog. I told them I'm moved by the little things people do to cheer themselves—little plastic Christmas trees in the gritty windows of walkups, an old man strolling in a museum with his hands locked behind him, a woman ordering jam for her bacon, a vivid young woman declaiming El Greco's use of color, a museum guard saying 'Hard questions, I want hard questions.' I just kept talking and pretty soon I noticed words in English and I started writing. I never got to go back. I was foolish to talk about the shapeshifting. I was just trying to make conversation, to make people relax a little and stop crowding me. That's how I ended up here."

His words fall down his throat and drown in a hubbub of sobs. Efrem pulls up a chair next to his patient, not in front of him but companionably beside him. He takes Marcantonio Whitman's hand, not like a doctor taking a pulse but like an older brother. The two men study the floor and weep. Then Efrem hands his patient the handkerchief Carmen always folds in sixteen squares.

"I think I can keep Rockwell and the others out for a little while, Marcantonio. Would you consider inviting me into the thirteenth world if they show you the way? Meanwhile we'll just encourage Mr. Portman's flu fears and tuna concerns."

Yo Scheherazade!

I left my first husband when it dawned on me I'd heard everything he was ever going to say. It took him seven years. He wasn't a total bore. What got me is he didn't even embellish what he'd said. I guess he didn't think I was worth entertaining.

I gave Hal, my second husband, fair warning. He was going to have to have something to say. Good looks, big bucks, great sex, fairy-tale children, nothing would avail him if he started repeating himself.

Little did I know that Hal Lanier was haunted by Scheherazade, who told stories to keep her wacko husband from killing her. Listening to him was better than sex. I had no complaints in that department either. It's not that all his stories were new—that's a bit much to ask—but they always got better next time around. Except one, and we almost divorced over that one.

I don't know what you think of a wife who demands such riches from her husband. But you show me a husband or a wife without a secret crazy button and I'll show you a mighty flimflammer. After you've lived with somebody a while you know just where his button is and the relationship depends on whether you respect him enough to keep your itchy fingers off it. It happens my nut button's toggled. Push it up, you find out how I despise knife-in-the-shower flicks, operatic car phones, dancing credit cards, yakky gas pumps and such like. Push it down, you switch on my evil intolerance of people who repeat themselves.

So why was it, I wondered in the sixteenth year of our marriage, that Hal pushed my toggle down every time he returned to the subject of his great buddy Owen Roundtree and the sinkhole? The story just hung there like a glass-eyed marlin in a Moose lodge. I owe him my life, he'd say in hushed tones. They were canoeing in the salt flats around Point Judith, Rhode Island, as young reporters and drunks. Then they got stuck, and Hal got out to push, only the muck started to suck him down and he thought he'd die like a stoned actor in a Grade B movie. But his great friend Owen kept his cool and pulled him out.

I hated that damned story ever since Owen Roundtree put his hand on my thigh while Hal was rehearsing a sober life. I hated it before that, actually. I hated it ever since the day I met Owen and looked into his moray eyes and felt like I was groping for a light switch in a dank room.

I'm telling you, Hal Lanier, you're either going to tell me that story differently or I'm going to leave you. He knew I would, not because I had a lick left of what once passed for sexiness, but because he knew I knew there was something fishier than all the salt flats of Narragansett Bay about that story. You must never lose your credibility in a marriage or anything else. It didn't matter whether my bags were packed or not, I would leave and he knew it.

"When I started to get sucked down into that mud Owen was sniggering like Peter Lorre," Hal finally told me. When I say finally, I mean he waited till I had my bags packed in my head.

"Owen told me not to panic. Then he laughed some more. He told me not to struggle or I'd sink faster. Then he opened another beer and started swigging. Then he started laughing like a tickled bear. He laughed so hard I thought he'd tip the canoe and fall in too. Which gave me an idea. I grabbed the gunwale and said, 'If I sink into this mud you're coming with me, you sonofabitch.' That's when he balanced himself athwart the canoe and pulled me up."

Hal Lanier never told me such a homely story in his life. He looked bereaved, like a sailor in a wind hole. Then nothing was the same. Yo, Scheherazade! But she was gone. I never said a thing about the sinkhole. We were taking our usual evening walk about a year later when he said, "The thing is, I've always pinned my life on somebody else. It's been a long wait for something to happen, some good piece of luck handed to me by the likes of Owen Roundtree, d'you know what I mean?"

"No," I said.

"I mean, I put my life in their hands."

"Their?"

"Yeah, people who see that you want something and act like maybe they'll give it to you if you live up to their expectations. That way my life is their lookout, not mine. Naturally they have to be deified. Owen Roundtree's a shit. I knew damned well something in that man wanted me to die that day. But I just kept on making him out to be my greatest friend."

"Why, Hal?"

"So I didn't have to be my own greatest friend, being so unworthy, you know. If he failed, well, he's somebody else. But if I failed, well, where'd I be?"

Right here telling me the story, I guess.

"We had all this time invested as drinking buddies. Course you and I know drinking buddies aren't buddies at all. They're co-conspirators. They go on imagining they've had these transcendent exchanges when all they've had is the mumbles."

That's all he said. He was approaching the problem archaeologically, digging gingerly, whisking things off, cleaning and gluing them. I'd have had more information if he wrote letters. But I knew it was a good thing, if only a beginning. Then Scheherazade came back and inhabited my old friend.

"Know why Alexander the Great is so hair-raising?" he said one day. "It's because he never waited for his ship to come in. He never waited for anyone, not Hephaestion, not Ptolemy, no one, he just went out and took what he wanted."

"What would Alexander have done that day, Hal?"

"That's like the Gordian knot story, isn't it? I don't know, but he wouldn't have done what I did."

Oh I don't know, Hal.

The Coots of Rondout

It's morning, April 10, 1997, when the vomitous azaleas start to bark. By one p.m. he hears whispering in his computer mouse. It's heavenly, that's the only way he can think of it. He desperately wants to make out the words. His life will prove worthwhile if he can. A monstrous tsunami rips protons and electrons off the face of the sun and hurls them at earth to disrupt its magnetic field.

Hoyt Coldrick sits in the newsroom cobbling wire reports into a coherent story. Then it will be melded with reports of local phenomena: power failures, computer craziness, fires, strange voices—anomalies, as the meteorologists call them. To do this familiar task, there's something he needs to remember, something he's forgotten. He grabs his lunch bag and goes for a walk.

Azaleas are still barking, yapping banks of terriers. He hates terriers. Then it comes to him: he can't remember a single movie he's ever seen. He remembers the names—*Das Boot, The English Patient, Twelve Monkeys*—but not a damned thing about them.

The spotty amnesia gremlin rubs out parts of your hard disk. You don't know what's lost. You bend down to tie your shoelaces and can't remember how.

He considers northerly climes where azaleas have to work to look so blowzy. How far north is that? And what if the mind isn't random about what it wipes out? Blessed thought. I don't need therapy at all, he thinks, I'll just wait and see what else has been wiped out.

Happily it turns out he can still tie his shoelaces and drive his nineteen-sixty-eight Pontiac Tempest with its third engine. Another good sign—he takes it as one anyway—is that he's forgotten some but not all of his newspaper skills. How to lay out pages, for example. Well, hell, he's been at it thirty-six years, long enough to see corporate looters destroy newspapering. He's seen them ghost newsrooms, pilfer pension funds, fire people on the eve of their retirements or catastrophic illnesses. He's had enough of the heartless bastards.

If he can't remember movies, so what? Read books? God knows he's got plenty of them. He and Petra spent most of their time and money collecting books. When Petra died of cancer her mother, Berthe, came with her ratty third husband. "I told her all that reading was bad for her," she said. When he got to the little stone chapel outside of town the sun was shining. The sexton had left a wheelbarrow by the cemetery gate. Just as the organ started triumphing Hoyt came down the aisle pushing that wheelbarrow. He shoved Berthe into it and carted her right out to the mailbox.

Now he has thousands and thousands of books and a queer hard disk. He eats his sandwich, goes back to the newsroom and cashes in his chips before the corporate bozos pilfer the paper's funds to buy another newspaper to loot and shut down for tax purposes.

All he knows is to head north to some place less hospitable to the damned azaleas.

There's a better chance of sailing Long Island to England than there is of paying the rent with the harebrained scheme he comes up with. But he can't think of what else to do.

Rondout, the old port of Kingston, New York, is one of the least likely places in the world to open a private library. Worse, what's a private library? He doesn't know. A handful of restaurants, galleries and dreamers are trying to restore the Rondout to its late nineteenth-century opulence, but the jury is hung. Things are so cheap, what with IBM pulling the rug out from under Ulster County, that even he can afford the old synagogue on Abeel Street. But he can hardly afford to fix it up, and he certainly can't afford the taxes, and the pigeons aren't giving an inch. His only comfort is that maybe he'll die before he has to pay the taxes.

He delights in Rondout's back streets. Their otherness—it is somewhere between sinister and lost to memory. There's nothing like it, except maybe those netherworld houses on stilts at Cape Hatteras in the twilight. Of course the waterfront, The Strand, is all gussied up with fairy lights. But the four- and five-story houses on the back streets crouch like crones down to the Hudson, and he spends endless evening hours up and down the hills wondering about the people who live in them and the people who used to live in them.

He starts with the roof, just to get his seven thousand books out of storage. The roof isn't too bad. Most of the fallen slates are still in the yard in one piece. He has no business at his age scampering about a peaked four-story roof, and that's where his walking around starts to pay off. He talks to most people he meets, people slouching on stoops or rotting porches, people under the hood in the street, people mooching leftovers from restaurants. Six months after coming to Rondout he knows just about everybody who is out of work or too sick and tired to work. Some of them start hanging around. He shares his sandwiches and soups with them, and pretty soon they start to help.

Kingston is a city where the junkyards outnumber the new businesses, so his new friends know where to get things. They have a high old time—no beer till nightfall, he tells them—until the building inspector arrives.

"I don't know if you're ever gonna get a CO for this place, but you need permits for what you're doing."

"What's a CO? What kind of permits?"

"CO's a certificate of occupancy. You gotta have permits to fix this dump up. Then you gotta have licensed plumbers and electricians do the work, either that or they gotta certify it's okay, which they naturally don't wanna do unless you paid 'em to do it in the first place."

Rudy Vernooy is a civil engineer. When he retired he took a job with the city of Kingston as a building inspector. Not too tough a job considering the sorry state of Kingston's economy. His forebears lived in the Hudson Valley long before the English,

145

but there are more Dutchmen underground nowadays than anywhere else in the Hudson Valley.

"Well, hell," Hoyt says, "you sure know how to make a fella's day. What with all that good news, I'm gonna have to go to an AA meeting so's I can make room in my head to take it all in."

He couldn't have said a better thing if he'd stayed up nights thinking on it.

"I sure don't wanna drive you to drink. My name's Rudy Vernooy. What's yours?"

"Hoyt, Hoyt Coldrick, and with any luck it'll take more'n you to drive me there."

"I'm one of Bill Wilson's friends myself, Hoyt. I get the feeling you're new in town, so if you're looking for a good meeting I'd be glad to take you. This job has the same effect on me. I suppose all these dang codes have a good reason, but the net effect is that the dirtiest sons of bitches pass them and nobody else can afford to."

They look at each other in the twilight, their twilight, and chuckle.

Winter sets in before Hoyt gets the main floor fixed, so he hunkers down in the basement with two Aladdin kerosene heaters. The Rondout freezes just after Christmas. He goes down to The Strand at night, eats hot chili at Rosita's and watches the skaters circle their bonfires. One night, just after he buries himself under a hill of blankets, he hears a voice.

"Hoyt! Hoyt Coldrick, you down there? It's Rudy Vernooy."

"Which code are you enforcing tonight, Rudy?"

He flashes a big marine half-mile lantern upwards. Rudy's blue eyes punctuate the head of the stairs.

"Y'ever go ice-fishing?"

"I have to?"

"Yeah, it's one of the qualifications for your CO."

The two men spend many a night seated on ten-penny barrels around holes in the ice. Hoyt buys himself an old pair of ice skates. "The Dutch have mostly been replaced," Rudy tells him one night.

Hoyt waits. Rudy likes to run his thoughts by the ghosts in his head. If you interrupt him, he shuts up. "The world's kinda like a washing machine, you know. Gets unbalanced. What with the hothouse effect, volcanoes, earthquakes, explosions and everybody's mean and negative thoughts, the poles are gonna shift, Hoyt. Then what, I dunno. There's too much meanness. It's gonna shift the poles. There's gonna be a magnetic accident."

Hoyt learned that as a newspaperman the less you say the better—makes the other fellow talk. Talkers never know where you're coming from or which end is up. He figures that if the world being like a washing machine has anything to do with the Dutch being usurped, Rudy will get to it.

"They're still watching us, you know. Over there in those trees. You feel 'em?"

"The Esopus, you mean? I heard they were bloody. I mean I read it."

"Bloody? More'n th' English? If it'd been up to the Dutch, they'd still be here, th' Esopus."

"Yeah, so would the artists in Woodstock," Hoyt says.

He's still waiting. He guesses Rudy knows he is. "Lotta Vernooys living under somebody's new house. But it wasn't others replaced them. No, it wasn't Rosita over there, or the Italians who run the concrete company, or the hippies and uppity New Yorkers over to Woodstock. No, it was pure damned greed replaced 'em. You know what color greed is?"

"I'd like to read auras, Rudy, but I can't."

"Just as well. Color of greed's red, white and blue. Same colors I fought under. You, too. Fought for the right of some damned soulless corporate raider to fire people and ruin families and break our hearts. What is it you like about Rondout?"

"Yuppies can't seem to rub off its downright spookiness."

"You notice that, do you? It's like if you look out of the corner of your eye real quick, it might not be Rondout at all."

"In the twilight, yeah."

"I drive around lot and I'm gonna tell you everywhere is beginning to look like everywhere else. Now I think of it, everyone is acting like everyone else. You build a house, you pay

147

a bunch of guys to run around in their pickup trucks all day. You buy a paper, you read what he said and she said, but you don't read how the advertisers and other corporate pooh-bahs are selling you poison, stealing you blind and exporting your job to Bangkok."

If he didn't like Rudy already, he does now. Hoyt spent too much of his life watching newspapers cover the hell out of government because they don't have the guts to cover the moneybags who really call the shots.

He wouldn't notice spring were it not for the flashing semaphores of mockingbird wings in flight. By the time the wet black branches of trees waft a warm green breath, Rudy tells him, "Well, Hoyt, if you can show me some proof the pigeons have deeded over the synagogue to you, I'll issue you a CO for the ground floor."

"I'll talk to them."

Next morning Rudy grinds up before dawn in a pickup that looks like he hammered it into a semblance of truckdom. He pours them some coffee out of a thermos. "I see you haven't got your quitclaim from the pigeons yet. You know, the Baptists owned this great ark once, but they gave it up before they could afford to have the windows changed, which is why it still looks like a synagogue. C'mon, get up, we're going shad fishing down to Edgewater. Ever eat shad? Almost as good as Hudson River sturgeon."

Hoyt looks glum. He didn't expect to survive the winter. Rudy is a pain for making him face up to what he halfheartedly put in motion.

A faint hope buds that he might surmount Rudy Vernooy's merciless optimism, even his connivance. This forlorn hope survives their rebuilding a junked van. It even survives their ferrying old folks to the library to browse, munch goodies, and sip tea and coffee and hot chocolate. He perseveres in his conviction that nothing after the deaths of Petra and the newspaper industry warrants another spring. His obituarial presence in Rondout remains triumphal.

148

Watching robins tug worms out of the sod reminds Rudy of Hoyt Coldrick. When it comes to that woebegone man Rudy has been pulling worms out of the sod. He sees that what they have in common is disillusion with sleaze. They have seen honor murdered on their watch.

Rudy is not only a recovering alcoholic, he's a recovering dupe, like most alcoholics. His daily rounds are a struggle to refrain from fondling the dupe's nostalgias. He misses the seductions of the flimflam, like the fellow who held out the promise of being his new best friend and then buried twenty-six septic tanks canted to flood the foundations of the houses they served. He misses the exhilarations of being courted by grifters. After all, they thought him worth the con. But he has come to know the hard way that once the con man is caught out he acts as if you smell bad, as if he's the aggrieved party, and he leaves you mourning his attentions.

Perhaps because his job is as bad for him as bartending is for a dried-up boozer, he's drawn to Hoyt Coldrick. Hoyt wants nothing. He doesn't even feel that the maintenance of a civil relationship with the building inspector is at least circumspect, and that's what tinges Rudy's warm feeling for him with indignation. The man has no right hauling books and griefs up from the south and seizing on Rudy as the instrument of his final undoing. No, damn it, the son-of-a-bitch is going to make something of his cockamamie idea and he's going to sit there on Abeel Street and live with it.

That's Rudy's pighead prevaricating while a metaphysical idea takes shape. Hoyt Coldrick put a vision in motion, seemingly setting it up to be kicked to pieces, but suppose something is going wrong with his formula, suppose Hoyt's vision wants to outfox its mortuarial inception? This is an idea a Dutchman born in the Catskills is bound to like: you build something contrary to the druthers of those mountains and they'll send it packing down to Mother Hudson some spring. Just maybe, this is not a contrary idea.

As for Hoyt, in answer to a prayer synonymous with his heartbeat that the Lord God Almighty, who allowed the

149

hypocritization of the business to which Hoyt gave his life, now allow the easier failure of his library scheme, the pestiferous Rudy Vernooy, that most sly of angels, has been sent to curse the ill-conceived scheme with success. Hoyt would have spotted him for his nemesis if Rudy hadn't seemed the perfect dream-killer: a building inspector.

He has to admit his own complicity. If it were going to look stillborn or pushed in front of destiny's truck, the scheme had to offer a few plausible ideas. One of these is that a geriatric population inured to the smiles of the alligators of Boca Raton might very well be in need of a hangout free of mall lizards. Libraries, Hoyt reasons to himself in the rare moments when hope, never as helpful as Listerine, rises like bile in his gut, are busy jettisoning books, organizing people who've had enough organizing, and catering to hordes of kids who'd rather make trouble.

So, once they get that van up and running, what with Rudy's forced intimacy with nursing homes and most of the codgers of Kingston and environs, the library on Abeel Street becomes a natural hangout. Folks come to read, to garden, to paint, to mess about in the huge kitchen, to play chess, to stroll down Broadway to the docks for ice cream, or burritos or a boat ride.

At first Hoyt thinks an annual fee—say twenty dollars—is in order. But Rudy has the idea of charging the nursing homes because he knows they're at wit's end to entertain their charges. Pretty soon eleven nursing homes are coughing up what they can. Seven churches kick in. Then the city and county human resources agencies. Then United Way. Before long Rudy and Hoyt are attending the Rondout Chamber of Commerce. They're heroes. Better yet, because Hoyt's so attentive during his evening despair pickets, the library's denizens are truly multiracial.

In May, the sun, poked and vexed by the Catskills, parts the buildings and burns antennae to find Abeel Street's white Star of David in its blue field. The two men stand aswarm with fairy dust in the choir loft behind the star, looking down on the white heads of their beneficiaries in the library below. They search each other's silhouettes and it crosses their minds that in this strange light a benediction has settled on their disappointments.

Later for You

"She's terrified. That's all I can tell you."

"You said the operation went well, so what the hell are you telling me, Doctor?"

"This is me, Chum, remember. Don't call me doctor just because I don't know what to tell you."

Francis Cholmondley (Chumley) went to Exeter and Yale with Tommy Scarpetti. They played squash together, got smashed together, rowed for Yale, but they were not equals, not in Chum's mind. Tommy was a pricey mechanic, and he had not done a good job fixing what Chum brought him to be fixed, namely Arleigh Waterman Cholmondley, his wife.

Nine days after her craniotomy at Columbia Presbyterian she was sitting up, nibbling solids and acting loonier than ever, which in Arleigh's case was downright eerie.

"D'you know who I am, Arleigh?"

"Yes, Francis, you're my husband," she said.

But she didn't act like she believed it.

"You sure she knows who we are, Tommy?"

"Well, if she doesn't, she's a helluva a mind reader."

What she was doing was cocking her head this way and that, like an osprey sitting on a buoy.

"What's that all about, Tommy? She acts like she can't see straight."

"Dunno. It may be an adjustment, synapses connecting. This is the brain, Chum. We know a lot, but there's even more we don't know. I told you it was a crapshoot. I think she's going to be okay, but we have to be patient." Scarpetti's awe at the mien, mannerisms and wealth of a Cholmondley had worn thin. The sorrows and deaths of others opened his eyes. Well, that's not quite true. He'd just been denying the witness of his eyes. That's why he visited Arleigh in her room more often than needed. It's true, she sits there, raising her wings in alarm if the boats come too close. He'd never thought of Arleigh as anything but a prize. Better than anything Francis Cholmondley deserved.

But it was a problem of symmetry. If you looked as good as Chum you had to have a wife who looked as good as Arleigh, otherwise it would just offend the order of things.

It takes six to eight weeks to recover from a successful craniotomy. The tumor was gone, the magnetoencephalograms looked good, but Scarpetti didn't think she should go home.

"You wanna go home, Arleigh?"

"I like your face, Scarpetti."

"What, you never saw it before?"

"Could be."

"What's going on with you, Arleigh?"

"I don't hold with all these new wave filmmakers, Scarpetti. I agree with John Ford, you've got to hold the camera still. The camera doesn't want to star. It has no ego. What's going on is I'm holding the camera still. Nothing to worry about."

"How come you're calling me Scarpetti all of a sudden?"

"I like Scarpetti. It's serious. You're a serious person. Look how you took this surgery. You didn't shit me about the odds, you talked to me like I'm a serious person. Now, Francis, he needs to be shitted. When you talked to me you said there was this little tumor in my Rasmussen's bundle. When you talked to Francis you said I needed brain surgery."

He tried but couldn't suppress a smile. He remembered she'd asked if he had ever talked to Rasmussen about it, since it was his bundle.

"You think maybe you can connect Francis's balls to his head sometime?"

Now he couldn't help it. Scarpetti laughed. The nurse came running from behind a curtain.

"It's okay, nurse, we're talking about the surgery."

"Yeah, that would be the surgery all right," Arleigh said. "See, if you did hook him up, Scarpetti, he wouldn't act like I'm bad brisket all the time, he'd just go out and fuck a buddy and leave me to my druthers."

"Or maybe not a buddy." Scarpetti was getting into Arleigh's mood in spite of the need for professionalism.

"Right."

He excused himself, but all afternoon he wondered about Arleigh's druthers. Over the sink, at the urinal, in the cafeteria. So before going home he looked in on her again. Her druthers looked all in place. She smiled.

"Not his mother, Scarpetti. Trust me, he knows what a shark's maw looks like."

"How did you know what I was going to say?"

"Maybe you left something inside my head."

"Maybe I didn't."

"Well, hey, you don't have to be a rocket scientist, right?"

"I thought you had a good marriage."

"Our parents like it. They don't fuck each other either."

"I never knew you had that kind of a mouth, Arleigh."

"C'mere," she said.

He leaned closer. She grabbed his white jacket and huffed into his face. "Sweetest damn breath you ever smelled, Scarpetti. Always has been."

It was. Stirring. Being bald emphasized her perfect bones and their mysterious shadows.

What he knew is that she knew he wasn't talking about her language but her mouth.

"So now we know there's no periodontal problem, you wanna go home, Arleigh?"

"Just as soon as I decide where, Scarpetti."

He nodded and started to leave.

"Hey, Scarpetti, don't go home and obsess about me, okay? Talk, don't obsess. I'm accessible."

"Are we flirting?"

"Wait till I get my hair."

155

Some damned thing is going on with her. I like it, he thought. I like Arleigh Waterman. Why the hell did she marry the guy? She'd always struck him as a little slow. Slow and armed against anyone's recognizing it by being elegant. Later, when he socialized with the Cholmondleys, if you could call being invited to Hastings-on-Hudson or Amagansett socializing, he'd decided she just took a long time to make up her mind about anything or anyone, which maybe is not quite the same thing as being slow.

Now she was souped up. Scary-quick. Christ, Scarpetti, you may damned well be a better a brain surgeon than you think. So now he too called himself Scarpetti.

He went home not exactly obsessing about Arleigh Waterman, as he preferred to think of her, but wondering if her kind of Waterford looks could punch his button if he let it. He never had let it because she and Chum always seemed a good fit, and since he was heading towards a life of logic and science, it made sense to honor the rightness of that fit. Something like that. But now he did remember one poolside afternoon, studying her mischievously prominent pubis borne like a silver chalice on some of the longest and best-turned pins he'd ever seen. It had to be silver, didn't it? She was that kind of blonde. And now he knew he liked her pheromones too.

"Arleigh, I think it's okay for you to go home now, but I want to talk to you about something," he told her next morning.

Her tailbone was jammed against the headboard. Her torso seemed elongated. Her head ratcheted incrementally like... not so much a bird as a blind person.

"Surgery is extremely traumatic. We don't even understand just how traumatic. You don't look the same, you don't feel the same, I understand that. But I'm just a mechanic, Arleigh, and maybe now you need somebody to share your thoughts with."

Scarpetti shared with her an inclination to think a long time before saying something. In him it was taken for manly taciturnity, and it had a kind of cachet. In her it was taken for emptiness.

"A shrink you mean. Of course, Scarpetti, my head is a bit swollen, isn't it?"

"This is a new lease on life. If somebody can punch your ticket, why not?"

"Validate it? Validate me?"

"Yeah, I think they use that word. Is it a bad word or something?"

"You're okay, Scarpetti. I'll think about it. I am thinking, you know. That's a good sign, isn't it?"

He squeezed her hand and she wondered why she'd never seen Thomas Scarpetti before. Here she'd gone and had her head examined, cut open and rearranged by him because he was Francis Cholmondley's pal, not because he was her pal, not because she'd checked his qualifications. It had been a long time coming now she thought of it. Having her head examined. That's what Francis told her to do whenever she said something zany. So what does she do, she goes and has it done by Chum's chum. Nice going, Arleigh. What a dutiful wife.

"Jesus Christ, y'know what I've done, Scarpetti? Let you cut my head open and play tiddlywinks inside just because you're Chum's pal, is that dumb or what?"

"It's seriously crazy, Arleigh."

They laughed.

"Ow," she said.

"Has it always hurt to laugh?"

"Get outta here, Scarpetti, what, have you got a thing for wigless mannequins?"

When she got home—a townhouse on the east side of Sutton Place between Fifty-Ninth and Sixtieth—Chum was downtown honing a suspicious new instrument called a derivative. He'd explained it at dinner parties and it sounded like a scam. Fact is she'd said just that the last time he told to have her head examined. She'd told him he was a throwback to his Rhode Island ancestors who got rich trafficking in misery and rum.

Maybe that's why the place didn't seem like home. She had the edgy feeling she'd come to the wrong place. Isn't this the place where she'd gone and done something dumb? Sure as hell felt like it.

157

Alice shot out from behind Huldah, their housekeeper, and bound her knees with her little arms. Arleigh put her hands on the girl's towhead and stared into Huldah's face. Huldah knew she didn't see her, not really. She had the bizarre sense that Arleigh was listening to the child through her hands.

"Huldah," she said. No smile.

"Mrs. Cholmondley, we're so happy to have you back."

She was a Prussian from Neuendorf on the Baltic. Austere, about Arleigh's age. She said she was glad to be in the United States but she lost no chance to greet the unfamiliar with her habitual dour look. Far from arming against Arleigh's stare, she returned it with a fey smile.

"Huldah, in the future I would be more comfortable if you would call me Arleigh when we're alone." She said it in perfect *Hochdeutsch*.

Huldah nodded, showing no surprise at Arleigh's fluency. She'd never used German to conceal anything while on the phone and she rather regarded this exchange as Arleigh's payback for Huldah's longtime certainty that her mistress ought to be taken more seriously than her master.

"Miss Irene is upstairs, Arleigh," Huldah said in German.

Arleigh smiled and went in holding Alice's hand. Irene's descent from the second floor was mannered. At the fourth step from the marble foyer she began nattering. She had, after all, supplanted Arleigh, so she felt she had something to be guilty about. Arleigh's stare silenced her. Alice could be heard somewhere ordering her ménage about like Frederick the Great. Huldah chose not to miss this encounter.

When the thirteen-year-old came within two feet of her mother, Arleigh put the side of her hand—observant Huldah noticed it was her left hand—to Irene's mouth like a priest in benediction.

"Shush," she murmured.

Then she drew the girl to her own girlish bosom and stared through the bull's-eye on the landing overlooking the East River.

"What's wrong?" Irene asked finally.

"Nothing, dear, nothing."

Alice liked her new left-handed friend. That's what Arleigh had always been to her, her friend. Huldah liked Arleigh, too. The coast at Neuendorf is haunted. Huldah had known changelings. But Irene was wary. She distanced herself from everyone. Arleigh thought that is what she ought to do, what would be good for her, because Irene had always manipulated people and hostaged their space.

They could not get Arleigh to talk against herself, over and against herself, and by her silences they were made to understand that that's what they had been doing all along, priming her to talk so that something inside her would be less formidable. Now she was quiet and formidable and took some getting used to.

"Could you turn the volume down, Chum?"

"Nothing's on."

"You're on. You're always on. It's your affect, Chum. You don't have to seduce everybody. Turn it down. Take a risk, maybe everybody won't like you, so what?"

"On? What the hell d'you mean on? What effect? What effect do I have?"

"Well, the effect is pretty overwhelming if you're insecure, Chum. But it's the affect I'm talking about."

"The what?"

"Your face is too bright. It hurts my eyes. You're in everybody's face. In their pants, in their pockets, what difference does it make? Relax, Chum. What do you need? Do you know?"

"Is this some Freudian crap? I'm worried about you, Arleigh. I think we need to get some other opinions."

"Oh, Francis, clamp your jaw. The operation is a success. Really. The patient doesn't poop her forty-dollar drawers or smack her lips or pick imaginary ticks or do anything to upset your guests. You're not sure, are you? Look, if it'll make you happier, I told Scarpetti before the operation that I wanted him to jury-rig my circuit board so I wouldn't do any of those zany Waterman things anymore. I told him the Watermans of Braintree are famous for dotty aunts, attic inventors, great American husbands who go out for a cigar and are never heard from again, and lactating mommies who initiate newsboys. Scarpetti, I said, see what you can do about rewiring me to make Francis feel secure in his investment. And I think he has, Francis. He is your chum, isn't he, Chum?"

She should look a bit Asiatic if she's going to wear a Cleopatra wig, he thought. He'd never let on he did have a bit of humor in him after all. Why hadn't he? he wondered. That really was a fine if disquieting speech she'd made. He'd enjoyed it, not that his torqued face would ever show it. He knew it might renew their contract if he would just show her how his mind worked. Now, for instance, it wasn't that he hadn't noticed the wig or appreciated its incongruity—those occulting northern eyes in that black helmet—it was just that they had a contract she was trying to breach and that wasn't done. He'd always found Arleigh funny, but it would bollix everything to let her know. She wouldn't know where to draw the line. It would get worse. Once in his study he'd even told a tumbler of Islay he'd tried so hard in the early days not to laugh when he screwed her it discouraged him.

She'd make the damnedest faces and noises. He knew, he did, that she'd love it for him to tell her. But then he wouldn't be Francis Cholmondley anymore and she wouldn't be... well, he didn't know what Arleigh was, Waterman being hardly enough to go by.

So, you going to or not? Tell her you've noticed the wig? No, he decided. She was just too much and always had been. And Scarpetti's fiddling maybe was going to keep her pants dry but clearly had inserted some foreign software. He would have to deal with her differently, but he kept on acting like a dabbler trying to get something up and running by Japanese-English instructions.

Had she asked Francis a question? She couldn't remember. Looking as if your fate depended on his answer was Francis's specialty, so Arleigh's interest had turned to Huldah or rather Huldah's death-defying Neuendorf ass as it appeared times three in Arleigh's triptychal mirror. She would like to entertain it in her lap. Was this too some of Scarpetti's tinkering? "Have you ever noticed Huldah's ass, Francis?"

"Oh for Chrissake, Arleigh."

He had.

"Well, I really think we should appreciate her more, Francis."

"You are frightening me, Arleigh, d'you know that?"

She studied him. "Yes, I think I can understand that. That's very generous of you, Francis, sharing that. I know you're frightened. I am too. Yesterday I really liked this new Arleigh. But today I know she's not going to stand still. D'you know what I mean, Francis? Round and round she goes, where she stops nobody knows. It is frightening."

"You off your pheenies, Arleigh?"

"Unh, unh."

He looked lost, the look she'd fallen in love with.

"We'll just have to see where Rasmussen sets his bundle down," she said. "Meanwhile, do take in Huldah's ass, Francis. It's really not to be missed."

"Okay, if that's the way you wanna be, later for you, Arleigh. The real world awaits." You count when I say you count.

Francis Cholmondley shuffled out of her bedroom looking dunked.

Arleigh looked up into the mirror over her dresser and saw Huldah smiling. Would the world ever get more real than Huldah's ass? Arleigh winked.

By late autumn she no longer looked like Frankenstein's bride. Her hair was long enough to quit Egypt and she looked rather like a gangly Etonian. The skeletal hand of a splotchy sycamore lifted the skirt of an awning as she loped down Sutton to Fifty-Third, where she would turn west and head for *Le Bateau Ivre* for lunch.

She'd been vacillating about seeing an eye doctor. When she glanced at Alice or Irene or Huldah or Francis they looked okay, but sometimes when she fixed each eye on the corresponding eye in their faces they looked different. At first she thought she was crossing her eyes. She put witch hazel poultices on her eyes and rested. She gave herself little tests, which she passed. Finally she decided to face the difference.

Alice shone with a milky light. A cerise penumbra pulsed here and there. Irene was wizened, dark, a crone scuttling in dry corners. It was Huldah who shocked her. She was a child. No, an infant held in a tender arm. Francis was rather a taupe egg, featureless, undeveloped. And yet the egg is perfect in its way, she thought.

Arleigh was just tetched enough by nature to stay out of doctors' offices and enjoy these matters as she'd enjoyed discovering the uses and preferences of her button. Francis had opined like a Jesuit after their marriage that its true consummation was to marry the money her grandmother Léonie had left her to his own. He'd opined in vain. Now she was determined he would not have the properties of Rasmussen's bundle, whatever they turned out to be.

She needed time to figure things out. Why, for example, when she put her hand on someone's head, or even their arm, did their words run away? Why in the space they abandoned did she hear other words? Words she wasn't ready to hear. Words that told her Huldah wanted to sleep with her, not as a euphemism for sex but just to hold her and be held. Words that told her Francis did not. He preferred to hold himself. Needed to, as any man born to such berserk parents would. Words that told her Alice had boundless love to give but Irene had questions. Why questions? What had happened to her? Surely not! The occasional temp, a pal's wife maybe, but not his own daughter. Still, the thought once born haunted.

She began to think of Francis as a taupe egg. She even remarked to her college roommate Dory Levine that he was a good egg. She began calling Alice babe and child. She treated Irene respectfully, her questions being worthy of answers. And she began to touch Huldah fondly as if she recognized the girl was lonely in her bones.

Never an addict, she now despised television, instead doing more than her share to support the literary fiction market.

She resumed running, sometimes up York past the Cornell Medical Center, sometimes west on Fifty-Seventh, the priciest street in the world, sometimes zigzagging all the way down to Union Square. People liked to watch Arleigh run. Bums yelled, Go, girl, go! Elderly gents doffed their hats or saluted her with their canes or umbrellas. Cops gave her thumbs up. Men with briefcases did double-takes. Her new self sometimes winked at girls, gaffers and men she thought deserved their good faces. Her stride was longer, her body fluid.

Once seated in *Le Bateau*, she ordered tea, took her bearings and ordered *salade niçoise*. The lunch crunch was over. She had seated herself in the window niche where she could watch passersby. Four suits came in and sat at the big round table nearest her. They had plenty of other choices, but she figured they liked blondes. The two swarthiest suits shouldn't have been double-breasted, not tall enough. The American came from Iowa or maybe Minnesota. His spiky brush cut looked hostile. A loose cannon, she thought. It was really the fourth man who intrigued her. Italian or Arab, Afghan maybe. Uncommonly handsome. His facial tissue all drawn theatrically away from his hawk's nose. His mien was severe, except that when you studied his face, humor radiated from the corners of his eyes.

Apparently they just wanted to breathe Arleigh's air, maybe sniff what she did for it, because they showed no further interest in her. The hawk noticed that she was listening to them and smiled innocently at her. She nodded with a smile and resumed picking at her salad. Perhaps her eavesdropping didn't concern them because they were speaking Arabic. She was sure it was Arabic. She often heard it on First and Second Avenues around the UN. She was picking at their words more diligently than at her capers.

The American was Karl. Her brain just didn't want him to be Carl. One of the two beeves was Tewfik, the other Mehdi. Now that was strange. Her insistence on the spooky one being Karl hadn't bothered her, but how would she know the beeves were Tewfik and Mehdi as opposed, say, to Toothpick and Meddie? She was not, after all, an Arabic speaker. Her exposure to that part of the world had been limited to *The New York Times* and John Le Carré's *The Little Drummer Girl*.

Well, perhaps she had read more, but certainly not Hourani's *History of the Arabs* or anything like that. And while she was dealing with this little nitpick she realized that the hawk's name was Amar. How the hell would she know that? Of course they must be using each others' names, but to pick them out and spell them seemed odd to her.

She listened some more. When she caught Mr. Amar's eye he looked almost jovial. She was now hearing another name. Hosain Ait Achmed. She knew something about this name. It was Berber, not Middle Eastern. That left North Africa. Then she heard, *I don't care, I don't give a damn, Hosain Ait Achmed is a dead man, you better make sure of that.* She dropped her tea into her *salade niçoise,* cup and saucer. Amar came from around Karl and handed her his napkin, smiling. He saw that Tewfik's words prompted her mishap. He asked her in Arabic if she spoke it. I am sorry, she said, and shook her head. She engaged him in French. That was a mistake. Of course a Maghreb Arab might speak French, so it hardly reassured him. She had overheard Tewfik. He knew it and didn't look so jovial anymore.

He returned to his chair, just once taking his eyes off Arleigh. Then he watched her as the men spoke. None of them raised his voice again. Arleigh paid up and left quickly with Amar's eyes on her. Thank God she had on her running shoes. She sprinted around Fifty-Second and took every turn she encountered, heading southwest, looking back every half block or so. At Thirty-Fourth and Sixth she hailed a cab and told him to go to the Metropolitan Museum. She could always calm down in Papa Corot's landscapes. She'd squat in his red soil, watching the sky boil over a green ridge.

You didn't have to be a spook to figure out that Amar, Tewfik, Mehdi and Karl were probably not going to be able to find her. She'd paid cash and Reynard Abril, *Le Bateau's* captain and the only person on duty besides the chef, was so protective of her that he regularly stiffed Francis. He was just one of the old men who innocently loved Arleigh on sight. So why worry? Well, for one thing, how had she understood the conversation? She'd begun to worry about that over her salad when she'd been rudely interrupted by Amar's attention. She spoke wonderful German. She spoke passing French. But her Arabic was limited to discerning it from Turkish or Farsi. She probably couldn't tell it from Swahili.

What would a Braintree Waterman do? You could get some shrink on East Seventy-Fifth to prescribe Prozac and pay for his kids' college or you could find out who Hosain Ait Achmed is. After all, Arleigh, you either heard it or you didn't. Since you did, who the hell is Hosain Ait Achmed and why does Tewfik want him dead? Well, there was a third possibility. You can find out more about Rasmussen and his bundle, but that would be a little like masturbating when you can't think what else to do. Arleigh usually had something else to do, but never say always, right? Besides, anything that made your nipples stand up couldn't be all bad.

"So Scarpetti, I want to know when I can start kicking some ass again."

Having dusted Huldah's arm as the housekeeper passed her on the foyer telephone, she wanted the doctor to tell her if she could resume her *capoeira* classes.

"How do you feel, Arleigh?"

"Crazier'n hell, Scarpetti."

"Are there any new symptoms?"

"Y'know, you're not entirely without humor, Scarpetti. The only really new symptom is I feel smarter, sort of. If you could do the same for Francis's Porsche he'd love you for life."

"Nah, he'd love me and leave me," the doctor said.

"Mmm," she mused.

"Tell me what you've been doing, Arleigh?"

"Everything?"

She enjoyed making Tommy Scarpetti blush and she knew he was blushing.

"I've been hanging around some dangerous-looking Arabs."

"How do you know they're Arabs? They tell yuh?"

"They might be Italians, actually."

"I think it will be all right for you to go to class, but talk to *maestre* and ask him to work up a fairly easy regimen for a while. Can you do that?"

"Sure. Nothing that'll land me on my head, right?"

"Yeah, something like that. Tell me why you're so wired. Have you done what I suggested? Did you see a counselor?"

"I think my endorphins are singing, Scarpetti. No, I haven't called what you euphemistically call a counselor. I've always been wired. It's part of my charm. But I did start thinking in the showers at college that it does more for women than men."

"Depressed men, Arleigh. Make that depressed men."

"Perceptive, Scarpetti, perceptive. But I attract depressed men. On the one hand I have all this energy for them to zap, on the other hand it's not exactly Siberian ginseng."

"Siberian ginseng?"

"An aphrodisiac, Scarpetti. They're afraid I'll electrocute them in bed or jump their bones and pile-drive them through the floor downstairs to where Mom sleeps."

"Jesus Christ, Arleigh, what're you on?"

"Arleigh Waterman's endorphins. B-y-e, Scarpetti."

"Doctor, conference call."

Carlotta Velez, the secretary he shared with Eos Christiansen, waited at the door. He was staring out the window and would have turned around and smiled except that his conversation with Arleigh had seriously embarrassed him, so he had to wait a moment.

"Hear ya, Carlotta. Be there in a minute."

Thomas Scarpetti was a solicitous man. He cared about people, but until now he had never craved to know what went on inside them. He was perceptive. He appreciated the differing natures of people. He valued their virtues, tended to forgive their failings, but he had never wondered day and night how a person thinks, feels, responds. He'd never thought about what prompts people to act. There was a culture, a code, the acceptable and the unacceptable. He liked certain men, loved his father and one of his uncles, liked certain women, loved

166

others, though not his calculating, wheedling mother. But he had never wanted to smell a woman, taste her, be a fly on her bathroom wall. Until now.

Christ, he told himself, just because you get into a woman's head doesn't mean you have to get into her pants, you know. But the crudity of the remonstrance upset him. That's not what drove him. It wasn't glimpsing a cheerleader's panties, testosterone refusing to go home, wham and scram, beaver shots, the whole jock gamut. Not at all. It was Arleigh's antic impulse, her humor, athleticism—it was Arleigh Waterman, a whole person who happened to be married to his erstwhile friend, for whom he now had terminal contempt. He'd been on the scent of this contempt for a while, he knew, but speaking to him of Arleigh as if she were a stock portfolio, as Francis had done, embittered Scarpetti. That was the right word, totally inappropriate to the situation. How could you deal with an Arleigh Waterman like that? See what you just did, Scarpetti? *An* Arleigh Waterman? We're talking about *this* Arleigh Waterman, the woman you happen to love. Got it, Scarpetti? It's called love. That's all. Just plain love. Albeit for Francis Cholmondley's wife. Thanks a lot, he thought. You couldn't arrange I should fall in love with a nice Italian girl, right? An Irish girl having always been out of the question as far as Papa Sal was concerned. Hey, how about even another WASP? An unattached WASP, I mean. A Korean girl maybe. A KGB turncoat, anybody! Dory Levine, Arleigh's buddy, she likes you, I mean really likes you. Smart girl. Rich family. Great bod. But the current's wrong. Hey, that's a good Italian marriage, right? Time to go scuba diving in the islands, Scarpetti.

Then who'd Arleigh call?

Arleigh was thinking in fast forward.

Why had she gone to The Met? The library was where she needed to be.

Looking for allies is a bad idea. Yeah, a bad idea. Besides, she'd always had lots of company, if only in her head. Arleigh was never lonely. If she didn't like present company, she just made up new company.

"Huldah, I don't want Irene roller-blading at night even if you're with her. You don't know karate. I don't want Alice talking so much to the doorman at Sixty South, the one who looks like a Transylvanian coachman, you know vich vun I mean?"

Huldah giggled.

"I'm going to be at the library. If you need me, beep. Mr. Cholmondley is eating with some clients and won't be home until about ten."

"Beep," Huldah said.

At the library she sat in a big green leather armchair trying to think what to ask the computer. Terrorists? Too broad. Her next-door neighbors were terrorists. Islamic fundamentalism? That's better. Wait a minute, Arleigh! Like you never went to college or what? How about Hosain Ait Achmed? Yeah, but I read the *Times* and I've never read anything about him. You read every little story with a North African dateline? Well, no. So tell the computer to look for Hosain Ait Achmed.

We got Hosains, we got Achmeds, but no Hosain Ait Achmeds today. We got Tunisia, we got Algeria, we got Morocco, but no Hosain Ait Achmeds who seem worthy of a hit by Tewfik, Amar, Mehdi or Karl.

Maybe it's the wrong newspaper. Could that be? If it's not in the *Times*, what would it be in? The *News*? *The Wall Street Journal* maybe? Not unless Hosain Ait Achmed was running a shady bank from Dubai or buying Philip Morris or... people are killed for much less.

Bingo! March 13, the *Journal* has a story with a Paris dateline about Elf Aquitaine, the big French oil monopoly. Elf is worried about *les intégristes* in Algeria, the Islamic fundamentalists. If they come to power, the country takes a hike back to the dark ages, Elf says, and there goes its investment in France's old playground. But down in the fifteenth paragraph is old Hosain Ait Achmed. Seems the Americans want the government in Algiers to hold talks with the Islamic moderates. What moderates? harumphs *Le Quai d'Orsay*. Well, yes, there is this old *caid*, one Hosain Ait Achmed, who talks of an accommodation.

He seems to have some influence in the Atlas Mountains, but not much is known about him.

Except of course that Messieurs Tewfik, Amar, Mehdi and Karl What's-His-Face want him dead.

Over morning coffee she called the Algerian embassy in Washington where she got the third secretary for cultural affairs. Her French was better than his English. They chatted amiably. He seemed in no hurry to brush her off. Then she asked as innocuously as she could if he knew who Monsieur le Caid Hosain Ait Achmed was. Quite suddenly he couldn't understand her pronunciation. She tried again but his selective hearing aid was on. She broke off, thanked him and hung up. Even a moderate fundamentalist would give Algeria's military government the jitters.

She called Professor Edward Said, Columbia's most famous Arab scholar, Palestinian activist and debunker of orientalism. Doctor Said picked up his own phone. Always a good sign. Indeed he knew who Hosain Ait Achmed is, but how did she know? Oh boy, this is gonna be good, she thought.

"Well, if you really want to know, Doctor Said, I'll just have to come see you. But if you're too busy, I really would appreciate knowing what you know about this man."

"That's impossible, Madam, I know too much to unburden myself on the telephone. May I know who you are?"

"Arleigh Cholmondley."

"I see. Yes, Chumley."

"Not like the bar in the village, it's spelled Cholmondley."

"Yes, yes, I like those names, Madam, like Featherstone-Hough"—he spelled it—pronounced Fanshaw. Well, I think we must talk. My last class is at three-thirty. Could you be here at four?"

Edward Said was a gracious and rather handsome debunker. The trouble was she had nothing to say to him. Unless of course she told him about the beeves, the hawk and the buzz cut. He was willing to talk about the *caid*, to a point. Arleigh, if nothing else, was pleasant to look at, so he talked until the pleasure began to make him feel a bit silly.

169

"Just what is your interest in Hosain Ait Achmed, uh..."

"Arleigh. Please call me Arleigh."

He smiled and waited for his answer.

That's when it happened. When they happened. Two things. She saw Said's real face. It was a boy's. A sweet boy's. And she heard what he was thinking. How interesting this woman is, how strange she'd call me out of the blue. I wonder what's going on. He was thinking what a good man might think. There was nothing to distrust.

"I heard four men talking about assassinating him."

She certainly had Edward Said's attention.

"It was in *Le Bateau*, a little bistro in my neighborhood. Their names were Tewfik, Mehdi, Amar and Karl."

"They introduced themselves?"

"No. I was eavesdropping. They were speaking Arabic."

"Karl was speaking Arabic?"

"Yes. Him too."

"I see. I didn't realize you were an Arabic speaker. Why didn't you speak Arabic to me?"

"I'm not, Professor. But I did hear them. I heard everything. Tewfik said Hosain Ait Achmed must be killed. Amar—he was very handsome—knew I'd understood. I got out of there fast and ran. I run."

"That would seem to be one of your least attributes, Arleigh."

"Look, I know it's crazy. You could humor me a few more minutes and then get rid of me and go on with your life."

"Yes, Arleigh, but then what if I pick up the *Times* and somebody has offed the venerable *caid* Hosain Ait Achmed?"

"Well, that's my problem, Professor. Maybe I should trust you."

"Have you any reason not to? You're not a Mossad agent, are you?"

"I had a craniotomy. Right here at Columbia Presbyterian." She paused. "Something about weirdy electricians rappelling in my Sylvian fissure."

Her literary idea of a populous brain amused Said immensely.

"Well, it was a success. Only now I hear people think and

170

I sort of see who they really are, what they're really like, or something like that."

"You hear me think?"

She nodded.

"Am I lewd?"

"Oh no! I would know. Really. Lewd's okay, though. I wouldn't mind. I'm kinda lewd myself."

"Well, in that case you definitely have me at a disadvantage, Arleigh."

"So what do I do?"

"Well, unfortunately it won't surprise anyone acquainted with the problem that a moderate has been targeted by hit men. The Arab Desk at the State Department might be interested. Then again maybe not. If things worked right I suppose they would pass it along to the CIA, which would alert the French and Algerian governments. But that may be a forlorn hope. Then there are the national and foreign desks at the *Times*. If they took you seriously enough to make inquiries, those inquiries might trigger something. God knows what! Don't say who you are to anyone. What else can you do? You can't tell them about Rasmussen. No indeed. You could live the rest of your life—I'd guess it's going to be a quite interesting life—without telling anyone about Rasmussen. I'm not sure I'd tell my husband if I were you."

"Especially not him!" Arleigh said.

Edward Said smiled. How nice it would be to have this lovely animated young woman in a class, he thought. She heard him.

"Actually I would like to take some of your courses."

He gave her a grave look, rose and offered his hand. She took it.

"Thanks, Professor, you've been a great help. I'll remember fondly that you took me seriously."

"Very seriously, Arleigh," he said.

She didn't know about Said's advice.

What did she have? The *caid* was a decent man. He deplored violence. He called for a Twenty-First Century Islamic state, *sharia* law, no usury, religious tolerance, altogether a benign vision. He declared that Islam abominated the killing off of the intelligentsia and foreigners. But who the hell was going to believe her? She didn't even know where the *caid* was going to be hit. What could anyone here do about Algeria?

Arleigh, this is all a ruse, a red herring to distract you from the real problem. Oh, how good that sounded! Right on target. But what in hell did it mean? Well, for one thing, it was certainly a problem sufficient unto the day that she heard people think. Any Seventy-Fifth Street shrink would be glad to make her a reservation somewhere out of harm's way on the basis of that claim. These voices, Mrs. Cholmondley, what do they say? They say Hosain Ait Achmed is going to be hit. Mmm, what else? Anything about your husband, your children? They say you're worried about your squash game. They say you're boffing your receptionist!

That's the real problem all right. That and a mind's eye that turns peoples' faces into mug shots and icons.

Wrong, wrong, wrong, Arleigh. The problem is not nuclear fission, the problem is fissionable people. What does Arleigh Waterman Cholmondley do when she doesn't like what she hears, loathes what she sees? Especially if it's in the head and face of loved ones. Well, Irene's a pill and Francis is a jerk, but I do love them, don't I? I mean I'd be a terrible person if I didn't, wouldn't I? It's your question, Arleigh. The thing is Irene has to have a mother's love to grow up straight and right. Like me. Sloan, Arleigh's mother, was certifiably batty, but she loved Arleigh dearly and showed it. So Scarpetti's rearrangement could not be permitted to change her iron-bound duty to Irene. Then there was poor Francis. He needed her to cheat on. She was dependable. Usually. Maybe not now. But she'd be so again. His clients always felt in safe hands when they met Arleigh. Nobody with a wife like Arleigh was going to cheat them or abuse their wealth. She wouldn't let her husband do it.

Do I know this? she asked. Yes, I know it. That's how those tax-cheaters see me. I'm Francis's bounden word. Did I always know this? Maybe, maybe not. So what's in it for me? I play with Huldah, seduce delivery boys, tickle my buttons in the bubbles, chop down a fellow Brazilian kick-boxer, study something

172

with that nice Professor Said, pour my affection upon Alice and Irene… What's that Francis says about derivatives? He's pushing the envelope. Yes, that's what I need to do. Push the envelope. Not under somebody's door. No, that's not what it means. It means have some respect for all those zany Waterman genes that have been waiting none too patiently to go where no one has gone before. I do not need a shrink to tell me who he is. That's what would happen, isn't it? I'd give him a hundred and fifty dollars an hour of Léonie's money to discover how bored he is and what a shit he is to boot. No, Onie, I will not do that with your money. There are women shrinks, you know. That is not the point. The point is Arleigh Waterman's got the bomb. Why bother to persuade anybody about it? But Arleigh, if you got it, flaunt it. Sounds good, smells bad. It's like old money. Don't show it. Don't prove it. Don't lose it.

Make a note, flowers to Onie's grave. She'd love this. Actually, Sloan'd love it even more. She could just hear her mother laughing musically up in the attic when she'd just made a few brush strokes on her canvas that she particularly liked. Arleigh, Arleigh dear, come up and see what's happened. Arleigh would race upstairs to admire her mother's work. Her mother would hug her and they'd go have lunch in the gazebo. Sloan had been content to paint all her life and never have a show. Make another note, have Sloan's work cleaned and reframed. It ought to be shown.

While she was waiting, *The New York Times*, in its passion to see significances before anybody else, reported that Hosain Ait Achmed was coming to address a human rights conference at the United Nations.

Arleigh clipped the story, yellow-marked the date, and reminded herself in her daybook to check the UN schedule the day before. Then she waited.

"Police tonight are looking for a tall blonde gymnast who apparently foiled an attempt to assassinate an Algerian religious leader on his way to address the United Nations. Channel Eight's Hot Eye News camera caught the amazing rescue."

The newscaster fell silent. Then he continued portentously. "Here now in freeze frames is what happened. Hosain Ait Achmed, surrounded by bodyguards and what may be Secret Service men or New York detectives, or both, gets out of his limousine. He starts walking on a blue carpet to the UN entrance when a Hollywood-handsome man steps out of the crowd with a machine pistol. You can see the security men reaching for their arms, but it looks like it's too late until a masked figure in black—they're calling her Wonder Woman tonight—flips out of the crowd head over heels and lands with both feet on the would-be assassin. He drops his weapon. He tries to get up on one knee. He reaches for his weapon. Wonder Woman whirls around and kicks him. Now she turns—notice how the security men seem stunned—flips twice, darts behind the limousine, rips off her ski mask, revealing a head of floppy blonde hair, and takes off. That's all the Hot Eye News camera caught. Police pursued her on foot, in cruisers and on horses. 'Boy, was she fast!' an exhausted patrolman Daniel Perchuk told Hot Eye's Maria Accamando. He said he and others chased her up First Avenue but lost her in Tudor City. 'She must have ducked into a service entrance somewhere,' Perchuk said. Police, using Hot Eye film, have put out an all points bulletin for Wonder Woman."

Hot Eye News didn't have the only exclusive. Police procedurals, Roseanne and Cary Grant, among others, were interrupted by footage showing Wonder Woman in her black Gore-Tex from various angles. She didn't deflect bullets with her bracelets, but she could have, no doubt. She was the talk of every bar in town. Preadolescent girls watching TV jumped up, pivoted and kicked their brothers. Adolescent girls in their rooms mimicked her in front of mirrors. A jaded city's imagination was jolted.

Wonder Woman even prompted Noemi Herrera down in Wall Street to ask Francis Cholmondley, "Just what am I derivative of?"

"The rich pleasures of conquistadors," he said.

Straddling him behind his desk, with her panties draped around her neck, she'd seen Wonder Woman save Hosain Ait

Achmed with the sound turned off. She let Francis finish—
Noemi was not mean—walked over to a pile of printouts, made
a paper airplane and flew it at him over his desk.

One of his more endearing qualities—even Arleigh thought
so—was that his testosterone did not work with crash test
dummies. He liked extraordinarily well-turned legs and brains.
Even better, he knew venality when he saw it—old money when
it gets very old is often blind to it—and he did not find it arousing.

For her part, Noemi accommodated her boss because she
thought a girl lucky enough to look so good owed it to herself
just to see what was so good about being Anglo that God had
blessed them so profligately. Knowing Francis as she now did, she
thought God ought to keep his eye on the game. Not that she
disdained him. Francis was not a bad lover and was a fair and
considerate boss. He was trying to fall in love with her, which is
why he kept money out of their relationship, but he did wish for
a bit more of the conquistadors and a bit less of their pleasures in
her, and she knew it. Far from pissing her off, it made her sad. She
was not unlike Francis. He did not like being tweaked by Arleigh,
he told her that, but he enjoyed Noemi's teasing. Perhaps because
she was of a lesser order, less formidable. That saddened her too.

"You're not rationing it, are you, Noemi?"

"Uh, no, I'm sorry, Francis. I got distracted."

"By what?"

How civilized he was. She liked that. It was hard to find
Hispanic men who would have let it go at that.

"I was thinking about your derivatives. They are a scam,
aren't they, Francis?" She didn't give him time to answer. "So I
wondered if I am too. I mean, am I a derivative?"

"You mean a substitute, don't you? A surrogate?"

"No, damn it, don't wag your native tongue at me, you
damned Anglo, you don't own it. I mean, do I derive from a
whole set of your hangups that have nothing at all to do with
me? You do get it, don't you, Francis? I mean, you do get me?"

"I take you very seriously, Noemi. I'm not trifling with you."

"Yes, yes, I know. Let's shut up now, I wanna see what's on
the TV."

175

The two had only to wait through one of Dixie Carter's monologues on *Designing Women* before Hot Eye News interrupted this program to take you to the United Nations where...

"Jesus Christ!" Francis said, zipping himself up, "for a second there I thought it was Arleigh."

He went over to a credenza to pour a big tumbler of Scotch. Always the gentleman, he offered it first to Noemi. She took it. He poured one for himself. "Did you see her? Was it Arleigh?"

"I didn't recognize her, Francis. I haven't seen her since the operation. Besides, all blondes look alike."

Even in his malaise he smiled. Both women were funny. His funny bone had to be engaged in sex.

"I guess I'm spooked. She's been spooky lately. What in the name of God would she be doing there?"

"Well, you live near the UN, Francis."

"We don't hang around ogling Arab wackos."

"He's not a wacko, Francis. Maybe Arleigh liked his face. She's funny that way, you know. She's been known to invite bums to your parties, hasn't she?"

"Mmm."

Noemi went over to him, put down her glass and held his sculpted face in her hands. "Maybe you're married to Wonder Woman, Francis. Isn't it thrilling? Who do you know who's fucked Wonder Woman?"

"What've you got down there in the bottom of those black pools?" he said.

"Currently, the hots for you. But that could change, Francis. You know that, don't you? I'm not for taking for granted, okay?"

"Okay," he said, feathering her moist crotch. "I don't, Noemi, trust me."

No, he didn't take her for granted, but trusting him was a whole other thing.

"Yes and no," she said, pulling down her panties again.

Arleigh saw twenty of her feet in twenty of Mr. Amar's wonderful faces in TV screens in Crazy Eddy's on Lexington. She frowned at her lousy flips and slow kicks. Since she was outside looking in the window she didn't know she was being called Wonder Woman.

After ditching the cops by wandering around in a couple of boiler rooms in Tudor City and snitching somebody's hot and crackling laundry, she headed for *maestre*'s studio at Thirty-Fourth and Lexington with her sweat suit rolled into her belt bag. There she polished her flips and kicks and did what she could to restore her artistic confidence.

She wished she hadn't whipped off her mask so soon, but there were thousands of tall blondes with feather cuts in Manhattan. Besides, the media would enjoy having this one on the loose. Maybe even the cops would. Maybe even Arleigh would. Then there was Edward Said. He'd call. But how? Their number was fashionably unlisted and Copleigh and Beresford down on Wall Street did not yet bear Francis's name, derivatives being a suspicious game.

The conversation she'd heard at *Le Bateau Ivre* was a diversion —an intriguing diversion from the real issue: what to do about Scarpetti's re-engineering of her brain.

When she left class, having bowed to *maestre*, she did something she liked inordinately. Waiting for the elevator, she bowed to herself in the mirror between the two elevators. Deep and formal. The Arleigh she saw was facing the issues.

If you were a telepath, or whatever, if you saw behind people's genetic masks, if you heard them think, then you couldn't get back to where you'd been, you couldn't be what you'd been. You'd get lost, you'd go mad. That was it, wasn't it? Trying to be normal makes you crazy. What's normal?

She didn't call 911. She didn't call homicide, the Arab Desk, the foreign desk, a shrink. She didn't try to talk, like she'd been trying to talk to Francis for fifteen years. Now why is that? If I can just make you see—that's what her life as a Cholmondley had been all about, just making somebody see. See what? That's what you do when *you* don't see.

Sweating out the toxins always felt good. Replacing them with endorphins was even better. But Arleigh was high on herself.

She'd done a great thing by keeping it all to herself. Whatever Scarpetti had done, or triggered, it didn't need confirmation. That's why Wonder Woman wore a ski mask.

She strode down Lexington, then turned west over towards Broadway. Her stride reminded Francis of a Viking ship. He'd never seen a Viking ship, except in the movies, but the analogy was one of his better moments. Actually she thought she was more like her grandfather's J-boat off Oyster Bay.

All the sunlight had sluiced off the streets into the Hudson by the time she found herself in the deep glass entry of Woronowski's Historic Instruments two blocks south of Grace Church on Broadway. Mr. Woronoski, who tuned their Baldwin, was working inside under a green eyeshade. She tapped on the door. The old gnome came to the door and peered into her face. "Missus Arleigh," he said when he'd opened the door, "what could bring you here in the middle of the night? You vud like a little tea?"

"With lemon, please."

"You are vell? Mr. Charlemagne is vell, yes?"

What Mr. Woronowski wanted, the thought that took shape as he put the kettle on, was that it would be nice if this beautiful uptown lady would just sit down in the corner where he could look over to her from time to time while he refinished Mrs. Herculomoff's Austrian zither. That would be nice.

Yes, it would, Arleigh thought, smiling at the old man. I'll just do it. She held his gaze and sat on a stool in the shadows. When the kettle whistled, he made her tea and brought it to her. "Mit lemon, Missus."

"Mit lemon, Levi," she said.

He was very happy. Life had been so eventful, the loss of so many people, the meannesses of so many others, why should he wonder what brought her here? What did it matter? If she wanted to spend a little time with Levi Woronowski on an autumn evening, what's to harm? Was it written in the heavens she had to be Mrs. Godalmighty Charlemagne on Sutton Place all the time? She couldn't be a little girl sometime? Maybe even Levi's friend?

Arleigh bathed in the humor of his thoughts. When he looked up—he had to lift his nose to see out from under his shade—she smiled and he went back to work refreshed. It was like his marriage to Lotte.

"You miss her, Levi?"

"Yes, but not so much as when I couldn't talk to her. It vuz crazy at first. Then I got so old it didn't matter. So I talk to her."

"And she answers?"

"Yah, but not like you and me."

"I understand, Levi."

"You vood. *You,* I mean. You understand?"

"Yes, Levi, I do."

He looked down to the zither and smiled. Then something came out of him unbidden. "You should come to see Levi more often, Missus. This is good for the soul."

"You're right, Levi. It's very good. I will. Could I play some of your instruments maybe?"

"You could play the archangel's harp, my dear lady. You could play Pan's pipes. You could play Gideon's trumpet."

She chose the viola da gamba and played a stately French court dance, a pavane. Levi set down his tools, wiped his glasses and sat with his hands folded. After a while she put down the viola, took a euphonium off the wall and produced its trombone-like sound and then its true baritone. Her Sousa march shook the shop. Levi rose and handed her an oboe. She played *Greensleeves.* Then a bassoon, then a mandolin. They could have continued, they knew. She sat with the mandolin in her lap, plucking. Levi returned to Mrs. Herculomoff's zither. She listened. He said nothing, not in word or thought. They basked in what had happened.

"I had an operation, Levi. The brain..."

Levi lined up four fingers before his lips.

"Lady, lady," he said, coming near, "ve hear vut ve hear, yah?" He put his left hand over Rasmussen's bundle in the cortex on his right side. "Dat's dat. Vut I think is you should come see Levi more often. Ve have tea and ve play."

"I'd like that, Levi."

179

She kissed him on both cheeks, hung up the mandolin and left. No moment in her life had been purer. Not Onie's or Sloan's kisses, not her first glimpse of Irene, not orgasm, first love or a black belt, nothing. She had been whoever she is without explanation and without it being explained to her. And whoever it was it was wholly accepted, wholly appreciated.

She glanced at her black Swiss Army watch. Eight-forty-five.

"I'll see if I can locate him for you," the nursing station in neurosurgery told her when she called. A few minutes later the voice said, "It's very unusual, but Doctor Scarpetti is scheduled to give a lecture in the amphitheater at nine-fifteen to some visiting Japanese physicians."

It wasn't hard to get into the amphitheater. She told them she was an interpreter and flashed her admission card to *maestre's* classes. Scarpetti was standing on an oval platform with a test dummy wearing some kind of frightening metal headgear. A stylus seemed to scribble on the dummy's head. On the other side of the platform was a computer.

When the Japanese guests had stopped their shuffling and coughing, Scarpetti said, "Welcome to virtual brain surgery. There are more synaptic connections than stars in the heavens. It will help to remember that. We make one-hundred-and-twenty-six cross sections of the patient's brain with CAT scanning technology. What we're after is a map of the terrain. Then, watching the computer terminal, we route the procedure. The image is accurate to one millimeter. We plot the trajectory of the invasion precisely. In other words, we practice. It takes less time in the operating room, it costs less, it's less intrusive, it has fewer complications. You're looking at the future of neurosurgery."

A hand shot up. Scarpetti waited. "This was developed here at Columbia, Doctor?"

"I hate to tell you, but it's a Gulf War baby. It was called dimensional imaging by the pilots. They used it to make virtual target runs. Their actual runs on Baghdad were just rote. But Columbia can't claim to have adapted war to surgery. Credit goes to the University of Virginia. We're just piggybacking. War

180

has always sponsored surgical advances. The American Civil War was pivotal. We're using techniques those poor damned battlefield surgeons in their butcher aprons developed."

"Where's my virtual brain, Scarpetti?" She ambushed him on his way to his office. "I guess you've got to go drink saki with the boys. Could we talk tomorrow?"

"Thomas, Arleigh, my name is Thomas. Tom is okay. Scarpetti is okay, too, if you want to keep your distance. You want to keep your distance, Arleigh?"

"Thomas, Tom, was that my virtual brain down there?"

"I've had a big research breakthrough today, Arleigh. I usually celebrate such things alone down at Raoul's in the village. Salvatore Scarpetti grew up down there, that same block, so I sit and talk to him. He pats me on the back and buys me Raoul's best wine."

"I'd like to meet him, Tom."

"C'mon."

Papa Sal was dead. Tom knew she knew.

"You gonna turn out the lights or something?"

He opened a desk drawer and took out a crumpled paper. He stuffed it into a pocket, put on a blue sailor's watch cap and peacoat, slipped an arm under hers and pulled her down the corridor. Outside he put two fingers in his mouth and let out a screech that stopped three cabs. Here was a Tom Scarpetti she'd never seen. Profane, unprofessional, street-savvy. She stood under the canopy studying him wryly.

"You gonna rent it or help this guy make a living?"

Another kind of Scarpetti for sure.

"I'm not exactly dressed for Raoul's."

"Trust me, if you're wearing it, it'll set a trend."

Levi would like Tom Scarpetti. Arleigh did.

"Dottore, I have a vino for you would make Mona Lisa weep. From Emilia Romagna." Then Vincenzo noticed Arleigh. "Such a lady, Dottore! Signora, *mi scusi,* but the dottore here is always alone. I am so pleased to see you."

"The maestro is worried about you, Tom. He thinks you're all work and no play."

"He didn't grow up down here."

"So did you make a virtual brain for me?"

This was not the way that she wanted to deal with Thomas Scarpetti. It was a defense. Nothing good would come of keeping him at bay. He'd told her that. He was a good sport. So was she. So was Francis for that matter. Is that why she was here, to quaff a little vino with a good sport? Is that what Wonder Woman, the handsome Mr. Amar's nemesis, would do?

"Tom, I have a secret I need to tell you."

He looked stunned. Or rather he looked found out.

"I know your secret, Arleigh."

"You do?"

She listened. She watched. But she received nothing except he knew her secret. She didn't send to know which one. For that reason what he said was a surprise.

He took out the crumpled paper and handed it to her. That was it, her secret on a piece of paper? A CAT read-out or something?

"Arleigh's Smile," it said. Then there were two columns of words and phrases side by side. The first said "open, friendly, intelligent, exciting, accessible, innocent, honest." The second column said "self-deprecating, embarrassed, secretive, haunting, wistful, otherworldly, fey." A diagonal line connected "exciting" with "self-deprecating." Another connected "accessible" and "otherworldly."

She kept her left hand on the paper and put her right hand on the side of his head. She closed her eyes.

"If they're not connected, they don't apply, Tom?"

"They all apply, Arleigh."

"So what're the lines for?"

"They're dry runs. See, this is a virtual smile."

CPSIA information can be obtained
at www.ICGtesting.com
Printed in the USA
FFOW03n0916200217
32548FF